A WICKED
TRUTH

Wicked Book 3

By M.S. Parker

Rom
Parker,
M'5
9-15

Copyright © 2015 Belmonte Publishing
Published by Belmonte Publishing.

ISBN-13: 978-1517251888

ISBN-10: 1517251885

3 6109 00488 6716

Chapter 1

"Shae Lockwood, you're under arrest for the death of Allen Lockwood. You have the right to remain silent..."

This couldn't be happening.

It had to be a dream. A nightmare.

Except I could still hear Detective Rheingard reading me my rights, and I could feel his hand on my elbow as he led me through the station over to what I could only assume was processing. Still, everything had that surreal quality I associated with dreams and nightmares. The way the faces around me blurred, how time moved in fits and starts, the heaviness in my limbs that made me feel like I was moving through mud.

I followed the directions I was given. Offered my hands for fingerprint scans. Turned to be photographed. I handed over my purse and jewelry, emptied my pockets. It wasn't until I was sitting in a small, windowless room that I realized they'd taken my engagement and wedding rings too. And that was when I realized I'd still been wearing them.

Even though I'd been widowed in June, and it was now almost Thanksgiving, I hadn't thought to take off my rings. Not even when I'd started sleeping with Jasper or after he'd moved in. And he'd never once suggested I remove them.

Jasper.

His name was like a punch in the stomach. I'd come to the police station because I'd found information that could possibly have implicated Jasper in the death of his best friend, my late husband. At the very least, it indicated negligence of some kind. I wasn't entirely sure what the legal ramifications were for having lied to a patient about having a terminal illness, resulting in that patient committing suicide, but there had to be something.

I'd come in on my own, brought Allen's medical records, as well as an email from Jasper to Allen suggesting a larger life insurance policy, and a letter I'd received from Allen a few months after his death. A letter that said he'd committed suicide due to the disease he'd been diagnosed with. A disease that Jasper had told Allen he had, but that the medical records I'd found proved a lie.

Instead of answering questions about this new evidence, however, I found myself being arrested for Allen's death.

The only sound in the room was my finger tapping on the top of the table as I waited. I was usually a fairly patient person – to be a second grade teacher, it was pretty much a requirement – but the detectives who'd been assigned to look into Allen's death were definitely testing me.

I'd known they'd been suspicious of me from the first moment we'd met. At least, Detective Reed had been. When it had become clear that Jasper and I had been spending a lot of time together, that suspicion had grown. I'd told myself they'd only been doing their job. After all, when someone died under mysterious circumstances, the spouse was always the first suspect. And Allen having died while the two of us were sky-diving definitely fit under the "mysterious" category.

Everyone had assumed it had been an accident, that Allen's chute simply hadn't opened. I'd thought the same thing until I'd gotten his letter and he'd revealed that it had been intentional. He'd done it because he'd known that an insurance policy wouldn't pay out for suicide, and he hadn't wanted to live through the end his disease would've put him through.

Or, at least, I'd thought everyone else had assumed it was an accident. Now, I saw the detectives thought Allen's death had been intentional. I just couldn't figure out what sort of evidence they possibly could've had to convince them I was a murderer.

"Mrs. Lockwood." Detective Reed came in first, followed by the slightly older Detective Rheingard. The latter carried a stack of files.

I didn't return the greeting. In the fifteen minutes I'd been left in here alone, my shock had turned into anger. They could've just asked me whatever questions they had. I would've cooperated. They hadn't needed to arrest me, especially not in the middle of their squad room with everyone in the police department watching. It'd be all over St. Helena before lunch.

"I'm sorry about all of that," Rheingard said as he sat in the chair across from me. "Procedure, you understand."

In my head, I'd always considered Rheingard the good cop to Reed's bad cop. Now I was beginning to think neither of them had been the good cop to begin with. I bit back my sharp retort and didn't say anything. I did, after all, have the right to remain silent.

"What are these?" Reed pulled the files Rheingard had been carrying over to him. "A letter, an email and some medical records? You just 'happened' to find them and brought them in out of the goodness of your heart."

I struggled to keep my voice even as I explained, "I received the letter from Allen at the beginning of October. The mailman who brought it to my door apologized and said that it had been lost in the mail for months. I believe Allen meant for me to get it shortly after he died."

"But it's typed," Reed said. "How do you know it's from your late husband?"

"He signed it."

"He typed his name," Reed countered.

"What would be the point in someone else sending me a letter like this?" I asked, curbing the annoyance in my voice. "Four months after he died, and someone's going to make up a story like that? Why? To mess with me?"

4

"You have had a bit of bad luck when it comes to people lately," Rheingard interjected. "Legal battles with your in-laws, a woman claiming to have had a child with Mr. Lockwood, a fire at the vineyard."

He was right on all of those counts. Allen's family had been coming after me for inheriting Allen's trust and all of his property, but the judge had already ruled that the vineyard was mine. The trust was still being contested. The paternity issue had already been taken care of too. The man who was actually Jenny Vargas's father had the test results to prove it, and he'd filed for custody of the little girl while charges were being brought against Aime Vargas for extortion, among other things. As for the fire, well, I knew the Lockwoods had been involved in that, even if there hadn't been any charges filed yet.

"I don't see what a letter from Allen has to do with any of that." I crossed my arms over my chest, grateful I wasn't handcuffed and could fidget.

"If it's real, it would mean that you'll lose that million dollar insurance policy," Rheingard said.

"Maybe that's why you didn't bring it in to begin with," Reed put in. "You wanted to cash in that million dollars, and you knew that suicide would void the payout."

"Jasper Whitehall was Allen's doctor. I confronted him with the letter, and he admitted that Allen had been sick." My stomach churned when I said Jasper's name, but I was able to keep my face blank.

"Then what's this?" Reed pointed to the top file

5

on the pile. "Allen's medical records show that he wasn't sick at all."

"Which is why I brought this stuff to you," I said. If they would've let me explain all of this before arresting me, it would've made things so much easier. "I was looking through a box and found Allen's medical records. After I read through them, I began to suspect that Jasper had been lying to me and to Allen about Allen being sick. I remembered that I still had Allen's laptop, so I went on it and found that email from Jasper to Allen talking about the life insurance policy, and Jasper telling Allen that he'd find the money to start his clinic somewhere. After Allen's death, I found out that he'd left Jasper a million dollars from his trust."

Detective Rheingard leaned back in his seat and gave me a scrutinizing look. "How did you happen to be looking through a box of medical files? I'm assuming your new boyfriend didn't have them lying around."

Heat flooded my face, but I refused to look down. I hadn't done anything wrong. "Jasper left his father's practice and is starting a clinic. He brought home several boxes of things and put them in the study. I was helping unpack, and found the box by accident. I saw Allen's name and read the file."

"Home?" Detective Reed's eyes took on a light I didn't particularly like.

"Jasper is living with me at the vineyard," I said, lifting my chin. "Or at least he was until I confronted him with the file and the email. When he said he didn't know about either one, I kicked him out."

"So you're saying that the day we planned on coming to arrest you, you just so happen to bring us information to implicate your lover in the death of your husband?" Reed smirked at me. "Pardon me if I don't believe you."

"What reason do I have to lie?" I asked.

"To throw suspicion onto someone other than yourself," Rheingard countered.

"What happened, Mrs. Lockwood?" Reed leaned forward again, putting his elbows on the table. "One year of matrimonial bliss and you were already tired of your husband?"

I could smell his cologne from where I was sitting, and it made me want to gag almost as much as his questions did.

"Did he beat you?" Rheingard asked.

"No!" I stared at the detective, shocked he would even ask such a question. "Allen was a kind, compassionate man. He never raised his hand to me or anyone else."

"If he didn't hit you, what was it? Did he have an affair? Maybe one of those cute little workers at the vineyard?" Reed asked. "Did you catch them going at it in the office? Maybe right out in the open? Was that why you set fire to that row? Was that where they'd done it?"

My mouth was hanging open, but I couldn't seem to find the willpower to shut it. I couldn't believe they were asking this.

Reed kept going. "You'd only been married a year, but you'd been together for, what, eight years? That's a long time to only be getting it from one place."

"You're a pig," I snapped, face flaming. "Allen and I were happy together. He never cheated on me. We were going to start a family."

I waited for that last statement to hurt, but it didn't. Maybe I was moving on. Or maybe I couldn't feel anything but anger and shock at what was happening.

"If you were happy together, then why'd you kill him?" Reed asked. "Or, maybe you were the one sleeping around, and he caught you. Was that it?"

"I didn't kill my husband," I said. My nails dug into my palms and I concentrated on the pain to keep myself from slapping him. "It was either an accident or suicide, but that's your job to figure out. I just came in here to give you some information that might help with your investigation."

"If it was an accident or suicide, Mrs. Lockwood, then we should only have found Allen's prints on his parachute pack, right? After all, he's the one who packed it. That's what you said." Rheingard leaned forward now, folding his hands in front of him. "But we didn't only find Allen's prints. We found another set." He paused for a moment, smoky blue eyes studying me. "We found your prints as well. Would you care to explain that?"

Chapter 2

That wasn't possible. There had to be some mistake. I hadn't touched Allen's pack at all. Had I?

I racked my brains, thinking back to that day that I wanted to forget. I'd tried so hard to push it to the back of my mind that it was hard to focus at first. We'd gotten to the airport and he told me what he planned. We talked to the pilot, the videographer, and the instructor who'd be going up with us even though we'd both done it before. Then, I'd gone to the bathroom, and when I came back, Allen had been ready to go. I'd packed my own chute, and we'd gotten onto the plane.

We kissed in the air before...*it* happened, but had we touched on the plane? I couldn't remember. The only thing I knew for sure was that I hadn't sabotaged his chute, either accidentally or on purpose. He'd had his packed before I'd come out of the bathroom.

After I'd gotten his letter, I assumed that had been why he'd packed his chute when I wasn't there, so I wouldn't see him rigging it not to open. He had to have sabotaged it since he needed it to look like an accident. If he just failed to pull the ripcord, it

9

would've looked suspicious.

"Well, Mrs. Lockwood?" Rheingard asked. "How can you explain your fingerprints on your husband's pack when you told us that you didn't touch it?"

"I don't know." I shook my head, confused. "I didn't pack it. Maybe I touched it on the plane, like when we were standing near each other. I wouldn't have thought of that before. He was wearing it, so I wouldn't really have been paying attention to where I was putting my hands."

"You expect us to believe that the prints we pulled from the parachute itself came from you touching your husband's back while you were in the plane?" Reed asked.

Rheingard shot him a look I couldn't exactly read, but I got the impression that something about Reed's statement bothered him.

"I don't know how you found them," I said, trying to keep my voice level. "But I didn't touch that parachute." An idea popped into my head and it blurted out of my mouth. "Maybe Allen switched them."

"Switched what?" Reed asked.

"My pack and his. It's the only logical explanation. I wasn't even there when he packed his parachute, but I did pack mine, so my fingerprints would've been all over mine. If Allen packed a parachute, then switched my pack and his, my fingerprints would've been all over it."

Reed snorted a laugh and leaned back in his chair, crossing his arms over his chest. "You seriously expect us to buy that?"

"I don't care if you 'buy' it or not," I said back at him. "It's the only possible explanation." I was getting seriously sick of his patronizing tone.

"You think that sounds more logical than you wanting to kill your husband for his money?" Reed scratched his head and looked over at Rheingard. "I don't know, Anker, you think a jury will buy that load of crap?"

"I didn't kill my husband!" I snapped.

"You were wearing your rings when you came in, Mrs. Lockwood," Reed continued. "You don't think that's the tiniest bit inappropriate? Banging your husband's best friend while still wearing your wedding rings? Or did you think that people might talk if you sold them too early?"

"I think your line of questioning is inappropriate." I could feel tears burning against my eyelids, but I refused to cry. Not here. Not in front of them. "Do you think I want to believe my husband killed himself? That he *chose* to leave me, and to do it in such a horrible, vicious way right in front of me?" I leaned forward. "I don't care what you think you know, or what evidence you think you have, because it's never going to prove I killed my husband because I didn't do it. You could have a hundred of my fingerprints all over that pack and it still wouldn't mean that I'd done–"

I stopped suddenly when I saw Reed's eyes shift. It was small, but he'd clearly looked away. Then I remembered something I'd learned from watching one of those cop shows Allen always loved.

Police were allowed to lie to a suspect.

"There aren't any fingerprints, are there?" I asked softly. "Not mine anyway. You were trying to get me to incriminate myself or change my story." I shook my head, giving them both a disgusted look. "Well, it might've worked. If I'd lied at any point, or if I'd actually done something wrong. But I'm innocent, so there wasn't a lie to catch me in."

Reed and Rheingard exchanged glances, and I knew I was right.

"What will it take for the two of you to believe me?" I asked suddenly. "A written confession from my dead husband?" I gestured towards the papers in front of Detective Reed. "Oh, wait, you already have that."

"What we have is a letter you could've written yourself," Reed said. "Especially when we have a source who says that you sabotaged Allen's chute, and that you'd do anything to keep us from uncovering the truth, even making up false evidence."

"A source." I pressed my fingers against the top of the table. "Which Lockwood is it? May? Gregory? Or is it Marcus? Maybe they decided to get Alice in on the action? None of them like me and they have everything to gain if I go to jail."

"It's called an anonymous source for a reason," Reed snapped back.

"Faris!" Rheingard's voice was sharp and he glared at his partner.

Apparently, sharing that bit of information with me hadn't been a part of their strategy.

"Is this anonymous source going to testify in

court that they saw something I didn't do? In front of a jury. Under oath." I looked from Reed to Rheingard and back again. "I think you know exactly who this person is, but it doesn't matter if you do or not. We all know that they're not going to come forward, because they didn't see anything, and they're not going to risk going to jail for perjury. The reason they didn't see anything is because there was nothing to see."

If this was an ordinary case, they never would've been allowed to arrest me on the uncorroborated word of an anonymous source and I would've walked out of there as soon as I delivered my little speech. But this wasn't a normal case because the Lockwoods had a long reach, and Allen had been well-known and well-liked.

I also thought Detective Reed was just a dick.

I didn't walk out after my speech. No higher-up in the department came in and told the detectives that they'd gotten it wrong and that they had to let me go. Instead, I went over my story again. And again. At one point, I was pretty sure they had me tell it backwards. No matter which way they came at me, my replies stayed the same because I was telling the truth. They just didn't want to accept it.

I lost track of how long I'd been there. Without windows or my phone, it was impossible for me to know how much time had passed, only that it began to feel like I'd been in that tiny room forever. I knew that couldn't be true since, legally, they had to put me in front of a judge within twenty-four hours of my arrest, and since it was a Saturday, they were going to have to do it soon. The knowledge didn't help the time move any differently though.

I considered asking to use the bathroom, just to get a bit of a change of scenery, but I knew that the detectives – and anyone who happened to be on the other side of that two-way glass – were watching my every move. They'd look at how I crossed my legs, my arms. How I held my head and when I blinked. When I hesitated. How much I drank, when I drank.

At one point, I thought it might be a good idea to ask for a lawyer just to try to get things to move along a bit faster, but I knew as soon as I did that, they'd assume I was guilty. Not having one and continuing to answer their questions with the same information over and over was my best defense.

After what I assumed was at least a couple of hours, the door to the interrogation room opened and a sour-faced older man stepped inside.

"Mrs. Lockwood's lawyer is here."

I opened my mouth to say that I hadn't requested a lawyer, but then Savill Henley walked past the older cop and came to my side. I had no idea how he'd found out about the arrest, but I couldn't deny that I was relieved to see him, if for no other reason than I was glad to have someone there who didn't think I was a murderer.

"Mrs. Lockwood is done answering your questions. If you want to speak with her again, call me." He glared at the detectives.

Savill Henley was in his late fifties, with salt-and-pepper hair and the large build of a once-muscular man who was starting to go to seed. He was also a corporate attorney who dealt with business matters and had taken care of Allen's will and things like that. He wasn't a criminal lawyer, but he'd been there for me through the Lockwoods' attempts to take my home, and had dealt with the Aime Vargas situation. A murder charge would definitely be out of his depth, but he wasn't showing even the slightest indication that he didn't know exactly what he was doing.

"Your client is under arrest for murder." Detective Reed stood.

He was probably used to intimidating people with his badge and the fact that his stocky build looked quite solid, but Henley towered over the younger man by more than a few inches, and intimidation was a bit tougher when you had to look up at the other person.

"Not anymore." The sour-faced man spoke up from the doorway. "It seems that Judge Hanson felt that she'd been deceived regarding the evidence the ADA said he had against Mrs. Lockwood."

Detective Reed shifted in his seat.

"The judge is looking in to whether or not it was a misunderstanding or deliberate misrepresentation of facts on the part of ADA Kline."

I glanced at the detectives and Reed's ears were turning red. I hoped they'd do a thorough investigation, because I had a feeling my arrest hadn't been a mistake on the part of the assistant district attorney or the judge. It wouldn't have surprised me if Detective Reed had pulled that same "fingerprints on the parachute" lie to get an arrest warrant signed. I wasn't sure how much Rheingard had been in on it though. Either he was innocent, or was just much better at concealing his thoughts. It didn't really matter to me. All I cared about was that this was over.

"Mrs. Lockwood's arrest warrant has been voided," the sour-faced man continued. "She's free to go."

"Lieutenant," Reed protested.

"Watch it, Detective," the lieutenant snapped. "I want to see you and your partner in the captain's office. Now."

"Before you go," Henley said. He tossed three separate, folded sheets of paper. "One is a copy of my request for a third, neutral party to be called in to investigate the authenticity of the documents Mrs. Lockwood brought in. The other two are suits – one civil and one legal – against your department for your treatment of my client. Detectives Reed and Rheingard are specifically named."

"You can't do that!" Reed spluttered. "We're just doing our job!"

Henley leveled a contemptuous gaze at the detective. "I suppose that will be determined after the judge takes a look at the evidence you used to secure an arrest warrant for my client."

With the way Reed's face was coloring, I certainly hoped he didn't have a heart condition. The last thing I needed was for him to have a heart attack and try to blame that on me too.

"You're free to go, Mrs. Lockwood." The lieutenant didn't even look at me as I stood.

My knees popped and my legs were stiff as I walked past the detectives and out the door. I kept my head up as I walked out into the station, determined that no one would see how completely humiliated and upset I was about what happened. I wasn't about to give anyone the satisfaction.

My steps faltered only once, and it was when I was halfway through the station and saw who was waiting at the doors. I caught myself though and managed to walk right past Jasper without a word or a look in his direction.

Chapter 3

I didn't stop until I was outside in front of the courthouse. It was warm for this time of year, pushing the high sixties, and the people of St. Helena were out and about, enjoying the sunny afternoon. If I hadn't just come out of several hours of being accused of murdering my husband, I probably would've been just as enamored with the weather as everyone else. At the moment, it was little more than a distraction.

"Shae," Henley came up behind me.

"How'd you know to come?" I was pretty sure I already knew the answer, but I needed to hear it.

"Jasper called me," Henley admitted. "He said the two of you had a fight yesterday and he left. He came back this morning, saw that you and that medical file were gone. He called a friend at the county clerk's office who told him about the arrest warrant, and then he called me."

"Figures," I muttered. I closed my eyes and ran my hand over my face. "Did he tell you what we fought about?"

"No, but I'm guessing it had something to do with those files you gave to the police."

I nodded.

"I don't want to discuss them now," Henley said. "Everything was so rushed, and since this isn't exactly my forte, I need some time to look things over."

"I thought you said the judge invalidated the arrest warrant?" I couldn't keep the frustration out of my voice.

"Yes, but that doesn't mean the case goes away." Henley squinted up into the sun. "Why don't you come into my office on Monday morning and we'll go over everything. Can you go in to work late?"

"The art teacher has the elementary kids working on a project for Thanksgiving, so she'll have them for the first part of the morning." I made a silent note to thank Gina. I could arrange things much easier with Principal Sanders this way.

"I'll see you first thing then." Henley paused, and then added, "We'll get through this, Shae."

He gave me an awkward pat on the shoulder and then walked away. I felt bad for him having to get involved in all of this, especially since this wasn't the kind of law he generally practiced. He'd been so good to me over the last couple months, helping me deal with the will, the surprise insurance policy. He'd taken meetings with the Lockwoods and their lawyers where they basically treated him like he didn't know his ass from his elbow – as my mother had been fond of saying. Then he'd gotten involved in the whole paternity suit, and had not only managed to get it thrown out, he'd helped out the real biological father in getting things started to have custody taken away from Aime Vargas as well as getting criminal charges filed against her for extortion. He'd gone above and beyond, and now I was asking him to do it again.

If this thing didn't go away, I needed to make sure that he was comfortable proceeding alone. If he felt the need, I wanted him to know he could have me hire a criminal attorney to work with him. I just didn't want him to completely put the case aside. I was having serious trust issues, and he was pretty much the only person I felt comfortable having handle something this important.

"Shae!"

Speaking of trust issues...

My entire body tensed at the sound of Jasper's voice. I was tempted to run away. Well, not literally, but at least walk away at a brisk pace, pretending I hadn't heard him. My car was in a side lot at the back, so I knew there was a chance I could get to it before Jasper reached me, but if he decided he didn't care about running, there was no way I could make it. I was torn between my pride keeping me from sprinting for my car and having to face Jasper. To make things worse, there was a part of me deep inside that wanted to wait, wanted to talk to him. I missed him, especially after what just happened. He'd been there for me through everything else, and my natural instinct was to turn to him. But a larger part of me wished he didn't exist.

I was saved from having to make a decision when he was suddenly there, his hand closing around my wrist, holding me in place as he stepped around me so we were face-to-face, his muscular body blocking me from going around him. I could go backwards – I knew he'd release my wrist if I pulled away – or I could step out into the street, but those were my only two options for escape. The only other thing I could do was stand there and hear what he had to say.

"We need to talk." His voice was firm, but not angry.

"I'm not really in the mood." I kept my eyes straight ahead, which might have been a good way to keep myself from getting distracted...if it hadn't meant I was staring at his chest. He wasn't wearing anything particularly tight or sexy, but even his simple flannel shirt couldn't stop me from remembering his firm muscles and the light dusting of dark hair on his chest, how it all felt under my hands, against my cheek.

"Look at me." His tone softened. "Please, Shae."

I didn't want to, but I found myself unable to resist. I raised my head slowly until I was looking straight into his clear gray eyes. My breath caught in my throat and my heart began to pound. It didn't matter how angry I was at him. I still wanted him.

"Talk to me."

I pulled my arm back, and he let my wrist go. My skin was warm and tingling where he touched me, and I had to resist the urge to rub it.

"I think we've talked enough." I kept my face up, but my eyes slid away so I didn't have to see that earnest gaze.

"We didn't talk, Shae. You yelled and told me to

get out."

I crossed my arms and took a step back, needing to put some space between us. I could smell him, his spicy aftershave, the detergent we both used. And him. That scent that was just him, that could turn my stomach inside-out. That told me he was mine.

"Look, I don't even care that you read that file. I believe you that you didn't look at anyone else's. None of that is the point."

"Then what is the point, Jasper?" I pinched the bridge of my nose and closed my eyes. "Because I've had a very long morning answering questions about things I'd rather not think about. I just want to go home and try to forget all about this miserable weekend."

"I want you to listen to me." Frustration tinged his words. "I want us to find out the truth about what happened. The two of us. Together. We're stronger together."

He was right about that, at least for me. I was stronger when I was with him. But I couldn't be with him, no matter what I wanted.

"I gave the file to the cops. Along with the email you sent and Allen's letter."

"Dammit, Shae! I didn't send an email to Allen. Not like the one you're talking about. And I don't know what the hell was in that file, but it wasn't mine. I want to find out what's going on, but I need you to believe me."

I wanted nothing more than to tell him that I believed him, to ask him to take me home, and curl up in his arms and spend the rest of the weekend there.

But I couldn't. I didn't truly know who I could trust or what to believe. I'd trusted Allen for most of my adult life, and then I discovered that he'd lied to me about being sick. That he'd committed suicide. And I knew Jasper had lied at least about being involved in that deception because he'd admitted it. Part of me thought the fact that he'd admitted the first lie meant that I should believe him when he said he was telling the truth now. But I couldn't help remembering the other thing he'd kept from me.

For eight years.

I couldn't let myself think about that. It was too much.

This was all too much.

"I can't do that." I shook my head. "Please, just let me go."

"Shae," he started to protest.

I pushed his shoulder and felt him start in surprise. Then he stepped back, giving me a clear path. I didn't look at him as I hurried past, and I made sure I didn't touch him. If I touched him, it would all be over. One gesture like that, and I'd be completely undone. I needed to be away from him.

I wanted to look back at him, but I resisted. I kept my eyes on my car and didn't let myself go until I was safe inside. I put my forehead against the steering wheel and closed my eyes. I felt so drained. My muscles were limp, emotions wrung out. I didn't even have the strength to cry. I was tired. So tired. I just wanted to go home, and go to sleep. Sleep and forget about everything other than a few hours of blissful ignorance.

Chapter 4

The room was dark, but I could feel him there. I could always feel him. In my mind's eye, he was as clear as he'd ever been. Thick tawny hair, sparkling hazel eyes. He had a strong jaw, a lean build. I could feel his muscles beneath my fingers, smell the minty mouthwash he always used.

Allen had been my first lover. He'd taught me all of the different ways my body could bring me pleasure. He'd shown me how to make love, how to fuck. The difference between the two.

His hand slid up my side, fingers dancing along my bare skin. I ran my fingers through his hair as his mouth made a trail across my collarbone, and then down between my breasts. He pressed wet, open-mouthed kisses on my flesh, then closed his lips around a nipple. I moaned, back arching as he gently sucked on the sensitive flesh. It tightened and he flicked his tongue across the tip.

"I miss you so much," I whispered as he moved his free hand down between my legs.

I closed my eyes, letting myself feel his touch, feel his body. I had missed him. His finger slid into me, stroking my walls. The pull of his mouth went straight through me, making my core pulse with desire. I felt the pressure growing inside me, and knew he could make me come just like this, from only his finger and his mouth.

"What do you want, Shae?" Allen whispered against my skin. He blew gently on my wet nipple and I shivered. "What do you want?"

"You." I tightened my hand in his hair, pushing at his head, trying to get him to move lower. "I want you. Always want you."

He let me push him down as I spread my legs wider to accommodate his lean shoulders. He settled between my thighs, and his mouth took the place of his finger. His tongue danced there, dipping and licking at every inch of sensitive flesh. I moaned and writhed, trying to get closer, impossibly closer. I wanted him inside me, a part of me. If he was part of me, I could never lose him again.

"Come for me, Shae." He slid two fingers into me, curling and twisting them.

His tongue teased around my clit for a moment, and I whimpered.

"Come for me," he repeated. "I want to feel you come around my fingers, come on my tongue."

My free hand found my breast, fingers tugging and pulling on my nipple even as his mouth latched onto my clit. Pleasure coursed through my body, feeding the fire in my belly. He rubbed the tips of his fingers against that spot inside me and I came apart.

I was still coming even as he moved over me.

His cock slid into me with one long, uninterrupted stroke and I cried out. My nails dug into his shoulders as he began to drive into me with slow, steady thrusts, each one pushing me higher.

"I love you, Shae," he murmured as his hips rocked against me. "I love you so much."

"I love you too." Tears burned as they coursed down my cheeks. "I thought I'd never feel you inside me again."

"I'm so sorry, baby. I never meant to hurt you." He cupped my face between his hands.

"You left me." Even as I sobbed, my body moved against his, desperate for the feel of him moving inside me, the slow burn of pleasure building. "You left me."

"I didn't want to, my love." He pressed his lips against my neck, my jaw. "I never wanted to leave you. I wanted us to be together forever."

"Then why did you do it?" I looked up at him even though I knew I couldn't see him in the darkness. My fingers traced the lines of his face. I never wanted to forget them, never wanted to forget him. "Why did you leave me, Allen?"

"I had to."

I could feel his tears dripping on my face, mingling with my own, and still he moved, sliding in and out of me with perfect rhythm. I hovered near the edge, not so close that I couldn't think, but close enough that I knew he could push me over any time he wanted.

"You didn't have to," I protested. "Jasper lied. You weren't sick. He let you kill yourself. He took *you from me."*

"No, baby. You know he didn't." Allen rained kisses across my cheeks. "It was my choice. And I'm so sorry I hurt you. But you know Jasper."

"I don't want to think about Jasper." I slid my hands down his back to cup his firm ass. "I just want you."

"And I want you." He brushed his lips against mine. "Always."

He took my mouth as he moved faster. His tongue plundered, tasting, exploring every inch even as he drove into me hard enough to make me forget everything we'd been talking about. All I could think about was how he rubbed against me, how the base of his cock pressed against my clit, creating the most delicious friction.

I gasped and moaned, and he swallowed each sound. His arms slid around me, and he crushed me against his chest, his body covering every inch of mine. I was surrounded by him, full of him. He was in me, around me, filling me. I breathed him in, tasted him.

"Come for me one last time, my love." His mouth was against my ear. "I want to feel you come apart under me, feel you squeeze my cock until I come inside you. Let me come inside you one last time."

I squeezed my eyes closed more tightly. I couldn't think about it. One last time. I didn't want it to be one last time. I wanted to stay here forever, stay like this forever. When I'd married him, I'd thought we'd be growing old together, that I wouldn't have to worry about being without him until we were both gray.

"Come for me, Shae." He lightly bit down on my earlobe, and it sent me over the edge.

I called out his name as I came again, pushing up against him. He pushed deep, my name a groan on his lips as he spilled himself inside me. I clung to him, riding out the pleasure, desperate to keep him inside me, keep our bodies together. I never wanted to let him go.

As he rolled us onto our sides, I hooked my leg over his hip, pulling him closer. He reached out and tucked some hair behind my ear.

"It's time, Shae."

I shook my head. "No." I put my hand on his cheek. "We promised to be together forever."

"No, sweetheart." He put his hand over mine and pulled it down, twining our fingers together. "We promised until death parted us."

I winced.

"It's okay that you fell in love again."

"But, Jasper..."

He leaned forward and stopped a sentence with a firm kiss. "You have the best heart, Shae. You need to listen to it."

"But what about..."

"No." Allen was firm. "What does your heart tell you?"

I sniffled. "That I love you."

"No, sweetheart. You *loved* me. And a part of you always will, but it's okay that you love someone else now." He kissed the tip of my nose. "What does your heart tell you about Jasper?"

I didn't want to think about it, but I knew Allen was waiting for me to answer. "I love him." The words caught in my throat. "And he loves me."

"He does," Allen agreed.

"And he loved you."

"He did."

The truth hit me hard enough to make me gasp, and I knew it had been there all along. I just hadn't wanted to see it because I'd been scared. Scared of loving him. Scared of losing him like I'd lost Allen. So I'd pushed him away before I could get too close. I'd used what I'd seen as an excuse even though I'd known in my heart that something was wrong, that there had to be a better explanation.

"He'd never do anything to hurt you," I said.

"And he never would have hurt you, not for a million dollars. Not for anything." He brushed his hand over the tears on my face. "You have to tell him."

"I will," I promised. I wrapped myself around him. "But not yet."

"Yes, sweetheart." Allen grasped my shoulders and pulled me back so he could look at me. "It's time."

"No." I shook my head. "No, not yet. I don't want to lose you again."

"I'm already gone, Shae." He gave me a sad smile, and I didn't think about why I could see him now. I just wanted to stare at him forever.

"Stay with me."

He looked so sad. "It's time to say goodbye."

"I don't want to." I touched his lips.

"Neither do I," he said. "But you need to move on. Let yourself love Jasper. Let him love you."

Something inside me released.

I leaned forward and gave him a soft, slow kiss. Then I leaned back and met his eyes. I brushed my fingers through his hair and held his face between my hands.

"Goodbye, Allen."

I jerked awake even as I heard Allen whisper, "Goodbye, Shae."

My cheeks were wet with tears as I leaned back on my pillows. My heart was pounding, and there was an ache deep inside me. It wasn't the pain of loss though. It was something new, something different. It was something cleansing and freeing.

I'd finally let him go.

But that wasn't all I was feeling. There was something missing.

Someone missing.

And I knew who it was.

I rolled over and grabbed my phone. I didn't care that it was late, and I knew he wouldn't either. I dialed his number from memory even as I fumbled at the lamp.

"Shae." Jasper's voice came through after the first ring. "What's wrong?"

"I'm so sorry." The words were almost a sob. "I'm so sorry."

"Shae, love, talk to me." He sounded wide awake.

"I know you didn't do anything to hurt Allen. I

33

knew it all along. I was just scared. I shouldn't have looked in his file, and I definitely shouldn't have believed anything I read. I should have talked to you, believed you."

"It's okay." He tried to talk over me, but I wouldn't let him.

"No, it's not okay. You have every right to be furious with me, but I'm asking you to forgive me."

"Of course."

"Please come home." I rubbed the back of my hand across my cheek, but I hadn't been crying new tears. "Will you please come home?"

"Home?" The word was tentative.

"Come back to me. Come home." I swallowed around the lump in my throat. "I want you here. I need you here."

"Shae..."

"I love you, Jasper."

Chapter 5

I showered while I waited for him to come over because I knew if I didn't, I'd spend the entire time pacing. I twisted my hair up behind my head and pulled on my robe. My face was still a bit puffy from me crying and my eyes were red-rimmed, but I could see the difference in my reflection. I looked lighter, as if a weight had been lifted off of me, and I supposed, in a way, it had.

It wasn't only that the dream had made me see what I'd already known about Jasper, but that it had given me what I hadn't gotten. A chance to say goodbye. It didn't matter that it had just been in a dream. I had closure.

With that part of my life anyway.

There were questions that needed to be answered, problems that needed solving. I knew all of those things would still be there in the morning. I also knew that an apology from me and a declaration of love weren't going to magically make things okay between me and Jasper.

But he was coming home.

My heart gave an unsteady thump when I heard the car coming up the driveway, and I was almost at the door when it opened.

His hair was tousled, his cheeks unshaven. He had bags under his eyes, and he wore a t-shirt and sweats, both wrinkled, as if he'd thrown on the first thing he'd found. He stood there for a moment, looking at me, and then crossed the distance between us in two long strides.

He took my face in his hands and rested his forehead against mine. We stood there, not speaking, not moving, but I didn't need him to say anything right now. It was enough to have him here, with me.

And then he was kissing me, his lips moving hungrily with mine as he buried his hands in my wet hair, taking it out of the twist and letting it tumble over my shoulders. His tongue slid into my mouth, and I fisted my hands in his shirt, pulling him closer, needing him closer.

I wasn't sure when he undid the belt to my robe, only that I suddenly felt the cold November breeze against my bare skin as he pushed the robe from my shoulders, and I realized that the door was open. I didn't care. Not as long as he kept touching me. His hands were hot as they slid over my skin, a delicious contrast to the air.

"The door," I finally murmured as his mouth pulled away from mine to start kissing along my jaw. "Close it." I moaned as he nipped at my earlobe. "Someone could see."

He made a low growling sound in my ear and his hands settled on my hips, fingers digging into my flesh.

"No one gets to see you like this but me." His breath was hot against my skin.

My stomach flipped at the possessive note in his voice. "Then you might want to close the door."

I let out a half-strangled squeak as he swept me up into his arms. He chuckled and I wrapped my arms around his neck. He kicked the door shut, his laugh turning into a low rumble as I nuzzled a spot under his ear.

"I missed you," I whispered, running my fingers through the hair at the base of his neck. "I missed you so much."

He gently set me down on the bed, his eyes darkening as they ran down my naked body. He pulled his shirt off without a word and his sweats quickly followed.

Fuck. He wasn't wearing anything underneath.

Before he could say or do anything else, I was up off the bed and going to my knees in front of him. I heard him catch his breath, and when I looked up, he was watching me, desire clear on his face.

"I'm so sorry, Jas." I reached out and put my hands on his hips.

"Shae..."

"Let me show you how much I love you." I leaned forward, flicking my tongue across the tip of his cock. "Let me show you how sorry I am."

I didn't wait for him to answer or argue.

I wrapped my hand around the base of his cock and began to lick every inch of him. His skin was soft, salty, and perfect. He moaned even as his shaft thickened and my stomach clenched with pride. I loved that I could do this for him. To him.

A part of me wanted to lose myself in the feel of him, in his taste, his scent, but a bigger part wanted to stay aware of every moment. I wasn't doing this to forget or for comfort. This was for him, and I wanted him to know I was here – body, mind, and soul. The last little bit of Allen I'd been holding onto was gone, and I belonged only to the man in front of me.

When I took him into my mouth, he was already too large for me to have him all. My mouth worked up and down over the inches I could handle while my fist took care of the rest with firm, steady strokes that moved in time with my mouth. His hand dropped on my head, fingers twisting in my hair. The familiar little pricks of pain went through my scalp, and the heat in my belly flared. I cupped his balls in my free hand, caressing them before releasing his cock so I could move down to take other parts of him into my mouth.

"Fuck, Shae!"

His hips jerked as my fingers danced along his wet skin, my tongue busy rolling his balls before pulling them back into my mouth. I felt his body tighten, and moved back up to his cock. He was close, pre-cum beading at the tip of him, his flesh swollen and red. I wrapped my lips around the head and then took in a couple more inches. He was close.

"Babe, I'm close." He pulled at my hair, but I didn't budge.

The hand on the base of him moved faster as I began to suck on him, hard, fast pulls that made his hips jerk and his grip on my hair tighten.

"Shae, please, I can't..."

I didn't bother with a response, only applied more suction, squeezed him tighter. And then he was coming, exploding in my mouth, across my tongue. He kept repeating my name over and over like a prayer, and I swallowed every last drop. I kept him in my mouth, licking him clean until he began to soften, and only then did I let him slide from between my lips.

He pulled me to my feet, crushing me against him as his mouth came down on mine. There was no timidity or gentleness to the kiss, only want and need. His teeth scraped against my lips, then bit down on the bottom one, worrying at it before pulling it into his mouth, soothing it with his tongue.

When he finally raised his head to look at me, my lips were throbbing and swollen, my nipples hard points pressed against his chest. His eyes met mine as he wrapped my hair around his hand, and then he was breaking our gaze, using my hair to yank my head back. Lips and teeth and tongue were hot and sharp on my throat, fueling the arousal already burning inside me. One hand slid between us to cover my breast, his fingers squeezing, palm skimming over my nipple.

"Jas," I gasped as he bit down on the place where my neck and shoulder met. My nails dug into his upper arms until I knew I'd leave marks.

He moved us until the backs of my knees hit the edge of the bed, and then we were both falling backwards. He covered my body with his mouth still making its way across my overheated skin. My eyelids fluttered as he kissed the tops of my breasts and I wanted to push his head lower. The need for release was sharp, and I knew all of the wonderful things he could do with his tongue and fingers, but another part of me was stronger. Before I could let this go any further, I had to make sure he understood some things.

"Jasper." I ran my fingers through his hair. When he raised his head, I cupped his chin and pushed myself up enough to brush my lips across his. "We need to talk."

A wary look came into his eyes as he rolled off of me, and I hated that I'd put it there. He started to sit up, but I put my hand on his shoulder, pressing him back to the bed. I curled up against his side, putting my head on his chest and pulling his arm around me.

"You don't have to apologize," he said quietly.

"Yes, I do." I looked up at him, but his head was turned away. "Look at me, please."

For a moment, I didn't think he'd do it, but then he moved. His eyes met mine, but they were blank, carefully masked. I pressed my lips to his chest and his fingers twitched against my arm.

"I should have trusted you."

"It's okay," he began to say.

"No," I cut him off. "It wasn't. It isn't. I was wrong not to give you the benefit of the doubt." I dropped my head so he wouldn't see my lips tremble. "Can you forgive me?"

He hooked his finger under my chin, tilting my head until my eyes met his again. The mask was gone, and all I saw was emotion so intense that it made my heart ache.

"Always."

His arm tightened around me as a wave of relief rushed through me. Even after all that had happened in the past hour or so, a part of me had still been afraid that he wouldn't forgive me. I put my head back down on his chest and listened to the steady thump of his heart.

Finally, he broke the silence. "Can I ask what prompted the change?"

I pushed myself up on my elbow, putting my other hand on his stomach. The muscles bunched and jumped beneath my palm.

"Allen."

His eyebrows went up. "Excuse me?"

I smiled softly, but there was no sadness to it. "I had a dream about Allen. I got to tell him goodbye, and he told me what I already knew."

"Which was?" Jasper's finger began to trace circles on my breast, the gesture almost absent-minded even as it spread heat through my body.

"That I should listen to my heart."

"Mm-hm." His thumb brushed over my nipple. "And what does your heart say?"

"That you never would've hurt him or me like that." My pulse quickened under his touch, and I slid my hand further down his stomach. "And that I love you."

His eyes jerked to mine, and I saw a cautious hope there. "You don't have to say it, Shae. I'm here even if you don't–"

"I love you, Jasper." I pushed myself up onto my knees, and looked down at him. "I can't say when it happened, only that at some point during this whole awful mess, you went from being my friend to my lover to the man I love."

I reached down and brushed some of his hair off of his forehead before lowering my hand to trace a finger across his lips. He was so beautiful it almost hurt.

He caught my hand and pressed it to his mouth. "You don't know how long...how many times..." His voice trailed off, and he closed his eyes, the struggle written on his face.

It hadn't hit me until that moment what this must've been like for him. Not all the years he'd loved me in silence. Not him having to watch me marry Allen. I finally understood what these last few months must have been like for him. His best friend was dead, but the woman he'd loved for eight years was finally his. All this time, he'd been fighting his own guilt at having me, at being happy.

"Jas, open your eyes." I waited until he did before I continued, "You haven't betrayed Allen. Neither of us have. You never once treated me inappropriately when Allen was alive. You didn't take advantage of me after he died. And you didn't force me to fall in love with you. It's okay to be happy."

He stared at me for a moment, and then I felt the tension go out of him. He sat up suddenly, catching my mouth in a short, but searing kiss.

"I love you," he breathed the words against my

lips.

"And I love you."

His hand slid down to cup my breast, his fingers teasing my nipple as he nuzzled the side of my jaw. "Does that mean I can make love to you now?"

"Nope."

He jerked back, a startled expression on his face.

I grinned at him and pushed against his chest even as I threw one leg over him to straddle his lap. "I still have to show you just how sorry I am."

"Shae..." His hands went to my hips automatically.

He hissed as I reached underneath me, and found him hard and ready. I used one hand on his stomach to balance me, and the other to hold him steady as I began to lower myself onto him. I gasped as he stretched me, the pressure of him filling me almost too much. I rocked back and forth, easing him inside at a torturous pace. I wanted this to last, wanted to stay joined to him as long as I could.

I rode him slowly, enjoying every inch of him as I took him into me. His hands moved from my hips to my breasts, teasing my nipples with gentle touches and sharp tugs. Each time he tried to take control, I pushed him back. My mouth and hands explored the hard planes of his chest, nails scraping his nipples, lips and teeth sucking and biting at his skin until he swore.

I pushed back my own orgasm over and over, refusing to let myself come until he did. This wasn't about me. He'd taken care of me so many times, always made sure I reached my own climax before he even thought about his. It wasn't until I felt his hips begin to jerk underneath me, his fingers grabbing onto my thighs, that I let myself go.

My leg muscles were burning as I moved, but it only added to the intensity of what was building inside me. I moved my hand to the place where our bodies joined, and began to finger my clit as I squeezed my muscles around him.

"Fuck!" He arched up off the bed, driving himself even deeper than before.

Sparks flew in front of my eyes and the hand on his stomach curled, nails digging into his flesh. His cock pulsed inside me and I felt the warmth of his seed filling me. Calling out his name, I pressed my fingers against my clit and gave in to the climax that had been waiting.

I fell forward, and he wrapped his arms around me, pulling me tightly to him as we came. I pressed my face against his chest, shudders running through my body. I could hear him murmuring my name against my hair, but I was too far gone to answer. The physical and emotional toll of the past few days had taken me to the point where I was completely and utterly exhausted.

I was also content. Sure, there were still more things to deal with, but he was here, and we'd face them together.

Tomorrow.

Because tonight, I was going to sleep in the arms of the man I loved.

Chapter 6

Jasper and I spent most of Sunday in bed, alternating between making love and talking. Some of what we talked about was the sort of sweet small talk that couples make while basking in the afterglow of particularly good sex. Stories from our pasts that we hadn't shared before. Things that my second graders had done. Difficulties Jasper was having with getting the clinic up and running.

Some of what we discussed had to do with a future when all of this was over, but always done in the sort of abstract vagueness that kept it from being too serious. We loved each other, but I knew neither of us wanted to discuss anything intense today. So we stuck to the simple. Vacations it might be nice to take. Long-term plans for the vineyard and for the clinic. Some of the future plans were a bit more immediate, like the upcoming holidays.

I'd been trying hard not to think about them, but Thanksgiving was this week, and no amount of denial would stop the ads on tv or the traditional hand-turkey art projects my students would insist on showing me. What would be the hardest about it was that because of his rocky relationship with his family, Jasper had always been a part of Allen and my holidays, so having him here for Thanksgiving would almost seem like normal...until I set three places at the table instead of four. And that was only if my brother decided he was going to come. He was still being weird about Jasper. It would ultimately be Mitchell's decision though, and I was able to let it stay at that.

The one topic we avoided as long as we could was the whole legal situation. Finally, Sunday evening, as we soaked in the large tub in the master bathroom, I brought it up.

I told Jasper everything that happened at the police station, all of the questions and accusations the cops had made, as well as the lie they'd told about my fingerprints. He agreed with me that the 'anonymous tip' had most likely come from the Lockwoods or someone connected to them. Since we had no way of proving it, we just had to trust that the evidence the cops did have would prove that I'd had nothing to do with Allen's death.

The problem there was that the evidence now seemed stacked against Jasper. I knew it had to be only a matter of time before the detectives turned their attention from me to him. What we needed to do was find out where Allen's file had come from and the truth behind the email I'd found. Jasper assured me that if the cops pressed charges against him for lying to the insurance company, he was prepared to take the consequences. He was guilty of that part, after all. What he wasn't willing to do was be blamed for something he hadn't done. I didn't like the idea of him getting into any trouble, especially the kind that might take him away from me, but that was a worry for another day.

We fell asleep at some point during a follow-up conversation, and by the time I woke the next morning, Jasper was already gone. On his pillow was a scrap of paper.

Had to go to work early. See you at home tonight. Love you.

I would've spent who knew how long staring at the note, grinning like an idiot, if I hadn't remembered that I had an appointment with my lawyer before school. Principal Sanders had been fine with me coming in late, but I didn't want to drag it out any longer than I had to. Better to get things with Henley taken care of quickly, and then I could concentrate on containing the overly excited second graders who would most definitely be worked up about the upcoming activities and holiday. I'd have my hands full.

Henley was behind his desk, nursing an insanely-large cup of coffee, when I arrived. His secretary was still getting things settled at her desk, but she took the time to ask me if I wanted some coffee when it was ready.

"No, thank you." I gave her a tight smile. I'd probably end up running through somewhere to get something before I got to school, but too much caffeine and I'd be on edge, which was the last thing I needed.

"Did you manage to get any rest at all this weekend?" Henley asked as he gestured to the chair

47

across from him.

I nodded, my ears burning as I thought of what I'd done this weekend. I sincerely hoped he didn't notice my flushing. That was something I didn't want to explain.

He sighed and leaned back in his chair, folding his hands on his stomach. "Okay, so I was able to spend the rest of Saturday and yesterday making some calls."

"Which I really appreciate," I put in. "I'm so sorry you had to work on the weekend."

Henley waved a dismissive hand. "Allen took care of it."

My eyebrows shot up. "Say that again?"

"Oh." Henley's face flushed with color. "Shit." His skin went a darker shade of red. "I wasn't supposed to mention it. Sorry."

"Don't mention it." My head was spinning. "Let's go back to the whole Allen taking care of it thing."

Henley gave me a partial smile. "Didn't you ever wonder why you haven't been getting any bills from me?"

My jaw dropped and he chuckled.

"I didn't think so," Henley said. "Allen set up a separate trust for legal issues. With everything taken care of for increased rates, overtime, all of that, you'll be good for years. One stipulation was that when you needed me, I'd be there. No matter what time of day or night."

My throat tightened. Allen was still taking care of me, even now.

"Mrs. Lockwood," Henley began, and then

hesitated.

"Go ahead." The fact that he'd switched back to the more formal title told me it was something more serious.

"I know about the letter you gave to the police. The letter, the file, and the email."

My stomach knotted. Yet another reason I hadn't wanted anything to drink. "I'm surprised the detectives let you see them."

"They didn't." Henley shifted in his chair. "The police department has a bit of a...well, a leak."

"Shit," I muttered.

"You didn't go out at all this weekend, did you?"

I shook my head.

"Read the paper?"

I shook my head again, blushing even deeper. Jasper and I hadn't bothered with much outside of the bedroom.

"That's probably a good thing," Henley said. "There's no easy way to say this, but the media's got ahold of the story."

I closed my eyes. I'd thought things couldn't have gotten worse, but, apparently, I was wrong. Again.

"And they don't just know that you were arrested. They know about everything you gave to the cops too."

I let out a string of curses that I normally wouldn't have uttered in private, let alone in front of someone else.

"What do we do?" I asked, raising my head.

"First, I need you to tell me everything. Where

49

you found the file, the email, the letter." He paused, and then continued, "And if there's anything else you think I should know."

I nodded and then began to explain everything, starting with the letter, and what Jasper had told me about his role in hiding Allen's illness. Henley listened, occasionally jotting things down. He never interrupted, never made any indication of what he thought about anything I said.

I didn't ask him for his opinion either. I didn't want to know what he thought about Allen's suicide, or Jasper fudging the paperwork for the insurance company. All I cared about was that he didn't think I'd killed my husband.

When I finished, I slumped back in the chair, my head pounding. It had been harder than I'd thought to explain everything.

He was quiet for a moment, writing something else on his notepad, and then he looked up at me. "Is there anything else?"

"No." I rubbed my hand over my face. How could I be so tired this early in the morning? "That's it."

"Okay." He nodded and tapped the pen on his desk. "There are a couple other things we need to cover before you go." His mouth twisted like he'd tasted something sour. "The Lockwoods have talked to some reporters."

Shit.

I didn't curse out loud this time, but the situation certainly merited it.

"What are they saying?" I asked with a sigh.

"Aside from everything I'm sure you can imagine they're saying regarding your marriage," he answered. "They're also saying you're trying to have them framed for arson so you can avoid the court ruling against you regarding Allen's trust."

I didn't feel anything about the latest lies. No hurt. No anger. It seemed like I was finally beyond all of those things when it came to the Lockwoods. The realization surprised me. I'd spent so many years caring about what they thought of me that knowing I didn't care anymore was a new feeling in and of itself.

"Obviously, it's all them running their mouths," he said. "But I have a feeling the cops are going to try to use the accusations against you."

"Against me how?" I asked, feeling my stomach knot in concern.

"They want you to come in and answer some more questions." He scowled. "Detective Reed called me yesterday evening."

"What more can they ask me?" I rubbed the bridge of my nose. "I was there for hours. I told them what happened forwards, backwards and sideways."

"And now they're going to ask you everything again." Henley leaned forward and pressed his fingers together. "Probably a little less politely."

"They could be less polite than that?" I asked dryly.

"They could." His lips twitched. "And they will. They're going to keep at you, insult you, insinuate horrible things about you."

51

"More horrible than saying I killed my husband?" I reached for my purse and pulled out a small bottle of medicine. I popped two pills into my mouth and dry swallowed them.

"Until they figure out what happened, they're going to keep looking," he said.

"Unless they're so focused on me that they can't see anyone else," I countered. "That they can't see the truth." I sighed. "What do you think I should do?"

"I think you should go in voluntarily," he said. "Answer their questions. Don't give them any reason to say that you're not cooperating."

"Does it mean anything that the arrest was voided?" I asked.

He frowned and took a deep breath. "Unfortunately, no." He scratched his head. "Just because I had a judge who agreed that they didn't have enough evidence to justify an arrest doesn't mean they're going to let things go. They can still put things together and get some judge who thinks things look different. That's why you have to put it all out there. No surprises."

I sighed again, something I seemed to be doing a lot of today. "When do they want me to come in?"

"The sooner, the better," he said. "The longer you put it off, the more suspicious it makes you look."

"All right." I rubbed the back of my neck. "I'll go in after school."

"I'll meet you there."

I shook my head. "If I'm just telling the truth, I

don't need a lawyer there, right? Doesn't having you with me make me look guilty?"

"Most criminal attorneys would advise you not to say anything without them," Henley said. His eyes twinkled with amusement. "But Allen told me that it would be pointless for me to argue with you if something ever came up. He said you were stubborn."

I smiled despite the pounding in my head. Yes, I thought. Yes, I was.

Chapter 7

Being stubborn did not magically solve all of my problems.

Not that I'd ever thought it would. Generally, my inability to give in on a lot of things caused more problems than it solved. In this case, however, I'd hoped that it would help. If I kept my temper and continued to repeat the same information over and over, eventually Detectives Reed and Rheingard would believe me. Everyone knew that one of the reasons cops asked things dozens of different ways and hundreds of times was to try to trip up a suspect. Lies were always harder to remember than the truth, and since I wasn't lying, my story wasn't going to change. It was just a matter of out-lasting the interrogation without letting them get to me.

This strategy didn't, however, help me when I walked into the school and found a note on my desk.

Please come to my office when you arrive. -
Principal Sanders

I glanced at the clock. I still had a half hour before my students were due back so I left my purse and bag in my chair and headed down to the principal's office. Growing up, I'd never been the kind of kid who got in trouble often. Or ever, really. Mitchell had been the one who'd done stupid stuff. Got caught smoking behind the gym. Cut class. I'd nearly cried the one time my teacher thought I'd passed a note in class.

I had that same feeling of dread in my stomach now as I walked down the hallway. I could hear the other teachers in their classrooms, the murmur of students answering questions, laughing at something someone said. All of it was muted, distant. The clicking of my heels on the tile was louder, echoing in my ears.

I didn't remember the office being so far from my classroom, but it felt like it took me years to get there. Years during which I thought about how I was going to have to apologize for having to come in late again, how I'd have to make sure that it never happened again.

I'd known that I was on borrowed time when it came to how understanding everyone was being, particularly at work. Principal Sanders had offered me as much time off as I needed at the beginning of the school year and had even said he'd be willing for me to work part time if I'd needed to. I hadn't taken him up on his offer, but there had been a couple times since then that I'd called off. I hadn't thought it was a big deal at the time, but now it seemed like it had bothered Principal Sanders more than he let on.

"Shae." He met me at the door of his office, a plastic smile on his face.

That caught me more off-guard than the note had. I'd never been close to Principal Sanders, but more because he and I didn't really have anything in common than any actual animosity. We'd always gotten along well enough though. He was my boss, not my friend, but he'd always been polite, warm even.

All of that was gone now. He wasn't being rude, but it was clear from how he carried himself that something was wrong, and that something was me. His back was stiff, his expression stony. He didn't offer me a chair, or ask me to sit, though he did close the door behind us.

"Mrs. Lockwood, it has come to my attention that there are some things I need to address."

"Yes?" I clasped my fingers in front of me.

"It's come to my understanding that you're having some...legal issues."

I clenched my jaw to keep the polite smile on my face. Behind him, on the desk, I could see a copy of today's paper. Shit. I wondered if the Lockwoods' accusations were in there too, or just the fact that I'd been arrested and questioned in Allen's death.

"Yes," I agreed. "That's where I was this morning, speaking with my attorney. And thank you again for letting me come in late. I'll make sure all of my future appointments are done after school hours."

"I appreciate that," he said, with that same fake smile. "But that's a minor detail. I'm more concerned with the nature of your legal problems."

"The nature?" I frowned.

"We're not talking about a parking ticket, Mrs. Lockwood."

I really didn't like that he'd changed from calling me by my first name. He called all of the teachers by their given names unless they asked him not to.

"You were arrested on suspicion of murder."

"I'm aware of the charges," I said quietly. I could feel my temper starting to rise and had to fight to keep it down. I couldn't, however, stay completely quiet. "I was there when they read me my rights."

"You understand, Mrs. Lockwood, that when you became a teacher, you weren't only agreeing to educate your students, but to keep them safe and set an example."

Okay, now he was starting to piss me off.

"When your husband died and you started...*seeing* Jasper Whitehall, I made allowances for you. Mr. Whitehall didn't accompany you to any faculty functions and you didn't discuss your relationship in public, so there was no need to address it."

Now I was staring at Principal Sanders in complete and utter shock. Gina had been living with her girlfriend for years. The wood-shop teacher was fifty-seven years-old and had never been married, but always had women coming in and out of his house.

And my relationship with Jasper was a problem?

"And there was the incident with Aime Vargas."

While she had come after me in my classroom, it hadn't exactly been my fault. She'd been nuts, jealous of the fact that Allen had married me and not her. It wasn't like my actions had been the reason she'd put my students in danger, and I'd done everything possible to keep them safe.

"While I understood that the incident wasn't entirely your fault, the fact of the matter still remains that she did put your students in danger."

"And she's in jail, Mr. Sanders." I could hear the edge to my voice and worked to keep it out. Losing my temper wouldn't be a prudent thing to do at the moment. "With quite a few charges against her and an impossible bail, I doubt she'll be visiting any time soon."

He stopped smiling, his eyes narrowing. "And now I learn that you've been arrested for murder."

"The arrest was voided." My stomach was starting to churn. I didn't understand what was happening here. "And I didn't kill Allen. I didn't do anything to him. I'd never hurt him or anyone."

"I'm not saying that you did," Sanders said. His eyes darted back towards the paper on his desk. "But it's out there, Mrs. Lockwood, and that's what matters."

His words hung in the silence between us.

"What are you saying?" I asked the question not because I really wanted to know, but because I was tired and wanted it over with.

He took a deep breath. "On behalf of the school board, Mrs. Lockwood, I'm going to have to suspend you, pending the resolution of your legal matters."

I blinked. I'd guessed it before he'd said it, but it still came as a shock.

"We'll be putting you at half-salary during your suspension," he continued. "The other half will be kept in case of your return."

In case. That was the same as *if*. Not *when*.

"I understand." I heard myself saying the words, but I didn't understand, not really.

"I'll need your ID."

"Right." I unpinned the card from the bottom of my shirt and handed it to him. "I'll be going then."

"Mr. Russell will show you out."

Mr. Russell. From security.

I was still in shock as Principal Sanders opened the door and motioned for me to leave. Mr. Russell was already waiting there, his broad face blank. He walked with me to my classroom and stood in the doorway while I got my bag and my purse. Then he walked me to my car as if I was someone who shouldn't be here.

I sat in my car and watched him walk back to the school, but he didn't go inside. He was pretending to be looking at something, but I knew he was waiting for me to leave. I wanted to. I was just waiting for the world to stop spinning.

When it finally did, I started my car, and pulled out of the parking lot. I wasn't even really aware of where I was going until I was almost there. I pulled into the clinic parking lot and hurried inside.

"Mrs. Lockwood." Georgia Overstreet gave me her usual sickly-sweet smile. "How can I help you?"

"Where's Jasper?" I could feel my voice quivering and fought to keep it steady.

"Oh, I'm sorry, but Dr. Whitehall is with a patient."

I swallowed hard. "Please let him know I'm

here."

She glanced behind me at the waiting room. Only a couple of people were sitting there. Jasper had said he was only taking on some of his regulars until after the holidays when he'd start things up for real.

"Dr. Whitehall left specific instructions that he not be disturbed. For any reason. He's very busy."

"Just let him know it's me." My voice sounded small. "I really need to speak to him."

"Honey." Georgia's voice dripped sugar. "He did say any reason. Even you."

Even me.

"Oh." I twisted my fingers together. "Okay."

I turned, rushing away before she could see the tears pricking my eyes. I told myself I wasn't going to cry, that I was done crying, but it was a close call. All of the steel I'd had in me was gone. I just wanted to go home and sleep until Jasper came home. Then I could tell him about everything that happened, and he would hold me and talk to me. He would be there for me.

There was just one thing I had to do first.

I pulled my cell phone out of my pocket and dialed the police station.

"Detective Rheingard, please." He was still the lesser of two evils.

A moment later, he came on the line. "Rheingard."

"Detective, this is Shae Lockwood." I closed my eyes and prayed that I'd be able to make it through this without cracking. "I was supposed to come in after work today to speak with you and Detective Reed, but I left work early. I'm sick. Something I ate maybe. Can I reschedule for tomorrow?"

There was a pause before he spoke, "Of course, Mrs. Lockwood. Whenever you can."

I hung up the phone and tossed it into the passenger's seat. It wasn't even noon yet, and I was seriously considering having a drink when I got home. I let out a bitter laugh. Why not? It wasn't like I had to worry about getting up for work in the morning.

Chapter 8

Instead of wine or beer, I considered drowning my sorrows in the double-chip fudge ice cream Jasper had brought home the week before, but I had to admit, albeit reluctantly, that making myself physically sick wouldn't be the smartest idea. I didn't, however, want to just sit in the dark and think about the newest development in the horror that had been this past year. If I did that, I knew I'd end up back where I was right after Allen's death. I needed to do something that would help keep my mind busy until Jasper got home and I could talk to him.

As I pulled up the long driveway that led to my house, it struck me what a beautiful day it was. The perfect autumn day. Not too warm, not too cold. The sun was out and bright, the wind brisk without biting. This was the kind of weather that people who attended football games on Thanksgiving hoped for. Here, mingled with the scent of leaves was the heavy, ripe smell of the grapes. Harvest had come and gone a few weeks before, but the scent of grapes would linger a while longer, I knew.

Back in the summer, just after Allen died, I'd

taken a walk out in the vineyard and given myself heat stroke. I supposed, technically, I hadn't exactly been walking. It had been more of a waking sleepwalk. Hence the heat stroke and the nasty sunburn. Today, I decided, I was going to take another walk, or rather a run. I wasn't going to be stupid about it this time though.

I changed out of my school clothes, and into a pair of sweatpants and a t-shirt. It would be a bit chilly at first, but once I started running, I'd warm up. My hair went back into a ponytail, and I rummaged around in the back of my closet until I found a pair of running shoes.

I'd never been a huge fan of running, but every once in a while, I appreciated the way a monotonous physical activity could help clear my head. Sometimes, it was a nice time to think about things, but it could also keep me from thinking about anything. Concentrating on putting one foot in front of the other, the impact of sole on dirt, the warmth of the sun and cool of the air. Breathing in and out, the increase in my pulse. All of those things came in a rhythm that lulled me into an almost hypnotic state.

I ran between the rows, picking my way across the dead branches and leaves that had been left behind by the harvesters. Bees and birds buzzed in the vines and overhead, looking for the last of the forgotten fruit. Their noise blended in with the rest of the sounds of nature. From here, I couldn't even hear the occasional vehicle going down the road.

I wasn't sure how long I ran until I arrived back

at the house and saw that two hours had gone by. My legs were burning and I knew I'd be sore in the morning, but it had been well worth it. For two hours, I hadn't thought about anything beyond my next step.

Before heading upstairs to shower, I went to the refrigerator and pulled out one of the pre-prepared meals I'd put together the previous week. It took only a few minutes to dump everything together and stick it in the oven. It'd be ready around the time Jasper usually came home and I wouldn't need to do any additional preparation.

I allowed myself the luxury of a long shower, enjoying the way the hot water pounded into my aching muscles. By the time I got out, my skin was pink, my fingers wrinkled. Even though nothing had changed in my situation, I had to admit that there was something about intense physical activity, followed by a hot shower that just made me feel better.

That feeling lasted until the oven's timer went off, signaling dinner was ready, and Jasper wasn't home yet. He wasn't more than ten minutes later than normal, but he hadn't called or texted me to say that he was running behind.

I paced in the kitchen, purposefully letting myself fret over the meal rather than giving into the temptation to call or text him. Aside from the fact that I didn't want to risk him trying to answer while he was driving, I didn't want him to think I was checking up on him. After what happened, I was going out of my way to show that I trusted him.

And I did.

I didn't believe he was doing anything wrong. No, my mind was currently trying to come up with all of the possible ways he could have been hurt or killed between here and the clinic. A normal person would've thought I was being overly dramatic, but after everything that happened since June, I didn't feel paranoid. I felt more like this was the other shoe I'd been waiting to drop.

When my phone buzzed after nearly a half-hour of worrying, I felt like I wanted to throw up. As I reached for it, I reminded myself that if something had happened to Jasper, I'd get either a call or a personal visit from the cops. The fact that it was a text coming in meant everything was okay.

The message was short.

Something came up at the clinic. Be home late. Don't wait up. Love you.

Something came up.

Something more important than coming home to me.

I closed my eyes and breathed out slowly. Jasper was a doctor. Of course things were going to come up for him that were important. He dealt with life and death, permanent damage. I couldn't get angry at him for not leaving on time when I knew it had to be something important. I knew him. He wouldn't tell me not to wait up unless something bad had come up.

And he didn't even know about my day, so there was no good reason for me to be upset that he wasn't coming home on time. I was the one who hadn't called him or texted him about what happened. Even after Georgia had told me he was too busy to talk to me, I could've at least left him a voice mail letting him know that I needed to talk. It had been my decision not to, so I couldn't blame anyone but myself for him not being here.

I got up and wrapped up dinner. He'd probably get something to eat at the clinic, but the chicken could be reheated tomorrow. I could even have a bit for lunch. I wasn't going to eat anything now. I didn't have much of an appetite.

After tidying up the kitchen, I headed into the living room. He said not to wait up, but that had been because he thought I needed to get up for work in the morning. If I was going to have to deal with all of the bad that came from being suspended, I would at least enjoy the benefits, one of which was that I didn't have to worry about staying up late.

Still, it had been an eventful day and the moment I stretched out on the couch, I knew I wasn't going to manage to stay awake. If I was here, though, I hoped Jasper would wake me and we could talk then.

I didn't remember falling asleep, but I knew I must have since, one moment, I was in the middle of watching some medical drama about competing surgeons, and the next, I was jerking awake to the sound of the front door opening. The tv had turned itself off and the room was dark. I sat up, trying to shake the sleep off, when the room suddenly flooded with light. I blinked against it, waiting for my eyes to adjust.

"Shae?" Jasper was standing over me, a puzzled expression on his face. "Babe, you didn't need to wait up for me. You should've gone to bed."

I shook my head and swung my legs over the edge of the couch. I sucked in a breath at the pain that shot through my calves. I'd stretched before running, but sleeping on the couch hadn't been a great idea.

"What's wrong?" He crouched in front of me. "Are you hurt?"

"My legs are sore, that's all." I tried to smile, but I had a suspicion that it came out looking more like a grimace.

"Why are your legs sore?" He moved up to sit next to me on the couch. He looked tired, but not exhausted.

"I went for a run this afternoon. That's all." I didn't look at him. I rubbed my hand over my face and tried to pull myself together. None of this was Jasper's fault and I wasn't going to let being half-asleep drag my emotions to the surface. I'd had far too much of that lately.

"Shae, what's wrong?" Jasper's fingers curled under my chin, gently turning me to face him. "Talk to me."

He sounded so concerned that my resolve wavered. I sniffled. Dammit.

He folded me into his arms as I began to cry. Between sobs, I told him everything from what I'd learned from Henley to my suspension. I didn't include my trip to the clinic, not wanting him to feel like I was blaming him for being busy. He didn't ask any questions while I cried myself out. He just held me and let me calm myself.

When I was finally done, he spoke, "Can I ask you something?"

I looked up at him, wiping my hands across my cheeks. "Of course."

His expression was troubled. "Why didn't you come to me right after it happened? Or at least call me?"

I dropped my head, looking down at my hands. "I did come to the clinic, but Georgia said you told her you didn't want to be disturbed. That you were too busy to see anyone."

He cupped the side of my face and I closed my eyes, leaning into his touch.

"Babe, I'm never too busy for you." He kissed my forehead. "When something like this comes up, I want you to come to me. Even if I'd been with a patient, I would've come as soon as I finished."

I opened my eyes and found him watching me. "I didn't want to bother you."

"You're never a bother." His thumb brushed across the line of my bottom lip. "I just wish I would've known. Even if you'd wanted to wait until I got home to talk, I wish you would have told me. I never would've stayed late."

"Your work is important," I said.

"*You're* important," he said. His fingers pushed hair from my face, then lingered to trace an eyebrow, my cheekbone, my mouth. "You're the most important thing to me, Shae."

I leaned forward, tilting my head so that he

could close the short distance between us. His mouth was gentle on mine, lips moving softly as his hands slid over my arms and down to my hands. He threaded his fingers between mine, pulling our hands up to his chest. He held our hands there, over his heart, until he broke the kiss.

"You own my heart." He raised our hands, kissed my knuckles, and then put my hand back on his chest. "No matter what I'm doing, you can always come to me."

I nodded and smiled at him. My pulse was racing, as much from his words as from the kiss. "I will. I promise."

"Good." He smiled. He stood and used my hand to pull me to my feet.

I winced as my muscles stretched. "I didn't think I was going to be this stiff."

"Guess I'd better do something about that." He grinned at me, then swept me off my feet.

Literally.

I barely had time to be disoriented before I was snug in his arms, curled against his chest. Without another word, he carried me up the stairs and into the bathroom.

Chapter 9

"I already took a shower."

I wasn't entirely sure why I was protesting. There was no way Jasper was going to walk me into the bathroom and then leave me there. I had no doubt he'd join me, and while I loved having sex with him pretty much anywhere, including the shower, I didn't think my muscles were up for what that entailed.

"I'm not giving you a shower," Jasper said. He set me down on the seat of the toilet. "And it's not about getting clean." He crossed to the tub and turned on the water before looking back at me. His eyes were dark. "I'm going to make you feel better."

Well, fuck.

I started to reach for the hem of my shirt and, before I could move, he was there, kneeling in front of me. His hands covered mine.

"Let me."

I nodded and let go of my shirt. His fingers brushed against the skin at my waist and I shivered. His eyes darkened for a moment, and then his face disappeared momentarily as he pulled my shirt over my head. He tossed it onto the floor, then reached

71

behind me to unhook my bra. His fingers slid along my spine, tracing each bump before moving to my shoulder-blades and up. He pulled the bra straps down my arms, and my bra joined my shirt.

His fingers hooked under the waist of my pants, and I lifted my hips so he could pull those and my underwear off together. Even that little movement made my muscles protest. I'd definitely overdone it today.

"Which scent do you want?" he asked as he stood. "Rose or vanilla?"

"You choose."

It should've felt weird that I was sitting here naked while he was completely dressed, but it didn't. And while I totally loved his naked body, there was something to be said for watching the way his muscles bunched and moved under his clothes. As he bent over to pick up the rose-scented bubble bath, his jeans tightened around his ass and my stomach clenched.

Damn. I'd almost forgotten how much I loved just watching him move.

He turned around, a startled expression on his face when he saw me staring. "What?"

I flushed. "Nothing."

"No, something." He came over to me and held out his hand.

I took it and let him help me to my feet. The familiar scent of roses filled the air, but as he pulled me closer to him, all I could smell was him. Fuck. He smelled so good.

"I was looking at your ass," I blurted the words

out.

"Really?" He arched an eyebrow, a pleased smile on his face.

"Really." I smiled at him. "You have a great ass."

He slid one hand around over my hip and squeezed my ass. "So do you."

"I have a sore ass," I came back.

"Right." His smiled softened. "Into the tub."

He held my hand as I climbed in, not letting go until I needed to grip the sides of the tub to lower myself down. I sighed as the water closed over my body, and I sank down until it just reached my nipples. The bubbles frothed around me, hiding the slightly darker flesh as I settled. The water was the perfect temperature, almost too hot, but not so much that it was uncomfortable. I could feel it starting to work on my sore muscles

"Relax," he murmured against my ear. "Close your eyes."

I shook my head. "Nope." I reached up with one soapy hand and ran my fingers through his hair. I was feeling warm, and a more than a little sleepy. "I wanna look at you."

He chuckled. "You're loopy."

I laughed and nodded. "A little."

He reached out and ran the tip of his finger down my nose. "Close your eyes, baby. Let me take care of you."

"You are," I assured him as I leaned back.

I closed my eyes, a small moan escaping my lips as Jasper's fingers slid across my wet skin. He cupped my breast, then began to move his thumb

73

back and forth across my nipple. It hardened under his touch as ripples of heat and pleasure fanned out from that point, moving through me.

"Relax, baby." His voice was low, soothing. "I've got you."

His hand moved lower, trailing down my stomach until his fingers brushed against the thin curls at the top of my core. I spread my legs, wanting his fingers lower. He obliged, his hand sliding between my legs. Long, strong digits delved between my folds to easily find my clit.

"Ahh..." The sound came out in a rush.

His fingers worked over me with surprising gentleness, just the right amount of pressure to keep the heat inside me building until he moved his hand lower and slipped one finger inside. My back arched, hips pushing up even as his palm rubbed against my clit. His finger moved slowly in and out, a soothing sort of rhythm. When a second finger joined the first, the pressure inside me began to expand, pushing its way through my body.

"Almost there, babe," he said. He ran the tip of his tongue along the outside edge of my ear.

He curled his fingers, rubbing the tips against that spot inside me until I was writhing. Sparks of electricity were shooting through me, making my skin tingle and my muscles quiver. And then the wave came, pulling me under fast and strong. I heard the water lapping at the sides of the tub even as it caressed my skin. Jasper's calm voice vibrated in my ear, coaxing me, reminding me that he had me, that he was going to take care of me. The strength of his hand as he held me, drew me out of myself.

It was like nothing I'd ever felt before. This wasn't an explosive orgasm, the kind that took my breath away, and made me see stars. This was the slow kind of burn, the sort of flame that engulfed and consumed everything in its path, turning it to ash.

When I finally came down, he was still there. His hands were in my hair, washing it, fingers massaging my scalp. I made a pleased sound and let myself fall into that blissful relaxed state that came after a really good orgasm.

By the time he was done, I was already half-asleep. I barely registered him draining the tub and lifting me out, but I did somehow manage to stay on my feet while he dried me off.

He carried me into the bedroom and slid me under the covers. The sheets were soft and cool against my bare skin. I snuggled more deeply, expecting I'd be asleep before Jasper climbed in next to me, but when he settled behind me, I was still awake. Everything had that fuzzy, almost dream-like sense to it, but I was coherent enough to pull his arm more tightly around me and press back into his naked body. He was hard against my hip and groaned as I pushed my ass against him.

"Not now," he murmured, running his hand down my side and over my hip. "You need to rest."

"But you..." I wriggled, drawing a half-pained sound from him.

"Shh, baby." He wrapped his fingers around my

hip. "I'm okay. No guy ever died because he had a hard-on."

"I love you." I pulled his other hand up so that he was cupping my breast.

He kissed my temple. "And I love you."

Silence fell for a moment, but I didn't want quiet. I wanted to hear Jasper's voice.

"Talk to me," I said, my voice starting to get that thick sound that came before I drifted off.

"About what?" His fingers combed through my hair.

"Anything." I closed my eyes. "What happened that you had to stay late?"

He made a disgusted sort of sound. "Georgia."

I was suddenly much more awake. "What happened?"

"She was doing something, moving some filing cabinet or something and she ended up cutting her hand. Easily a two-inch laceration across her palm. There was blood everywhere, and she was freaking out. I had to get her cleaned up before I could even take a look at her hand. She needed stitches, and then I had to bandage her hand up. She couldn't drive home because I had to give her something for the pain. Then I had to go back to the office, clean up the mess there, and fill out the workman's comp forms."

Jasper's voice was flat, almost bored, and the stroking of his fingers through my hair was hypnotic. It should have made me want to fall asleep, but everything he was saying was having the opposite effect.

Georgia.

I should've known.

I'd never liked her, but I'd kept my mouth shut. She'd been with Jasper for a long time, and she'd been helping him at the clinic. While she'd been terse – all right, she'd been downright rude – with me, I'd borne it because I didn't want to be *that* woman. The woman who thought that every other woman wanted her man, that every little slight was due to jealousy.

I still wasn't going to say anything, especially not now, not when I was so emotional. My head was a wreck, and I didn't need to be thinking of anything that was just going to make things worse. I also wasn't going to say anything without proof. I'd learned the hard way that I had a tendency to jump to conclusions when I thought with my heart instead of my head.

I wasn't going to do that again.

I also wasn't about to let her get away with it if she was going after Jasper. I knew now that I wasn't going to do anything that could possibly make me lose him. I'd lost one man I loved. Jasper was going to be stuck with me as long as he'd have me.

With that thought, I firmly pushed everything else out of my mind. The slow, steady breathing behind me said Jasper had fallen asleep, and I was ready to join him. I could feel the exhaustion in my bones, and gave into it. There'd be craziness enough tomorrow, but tonight, I was clean, I was comfortable, and I had Jasper's arms around me. That's all I needed.

77

Chapter 10

Knowing I didn't have to be up for work always made it difficult to get out of bed. Having six feet of hot, muscular man wrapped around me made it even harder.

Pun definitely intended.

I woke up before the alarm went off, and Jasper's cock was hard against my ass. I couldn't help but wonder if he'd been that way all night. Considering the fact that he still had one hand on my breast, and the other hand had slipped down until his fingers were brushing against the curls between my legs, I thought it was a good possibility.

Warmth filled me as I remembered what happened last night. Not all of the bad stuff, but rather the good. All the good that had come from Jasper. How he'd taken care of me. How he'd denied what his body so clearly wanted simply because he knew I was too tired.

Well, I wasn't too tired now.

I shifted, rolling over until I was facing him. His embrace loosened, and he rolled onto his back. I kept my eyes on his face as I folded back the blanket, but his eyelids didn't so much as flicker.

My muscles were stiff as I moved onto my knees, but I wasn't even close to how bad I feared I'd be. I knew a lot of that had to do with the hot bath Jasper had gotten me into last night. That and the very relaxing orgasm he'd given me.

Now it was time to return the favor. I let my gaze move from his handsome face, down over his amazing body. Broad, muscular shoulders and chest. Trim waist and hips. An absolutely beautiful, long, thick cock that was currently curving up towards his flat stomach.

And he was all mine.

I leaned down and wrapped my hand around him, holding him as I worked my mouth over the soft skin. I didn't look up when I felt him wake, felt the muscles in his stomach tense as he realized what I was doing. He said my name, but I kept my attention on the pulsing flesh between my lips.

It wasn't until I felt his hand in my hair, tugging me off of him, that I raised my head. I looked up at him as I let his cock fall from between my lips. My eyes locked with his and I moved my hand faster, gripping him harder.

"Shae, let me..."

"No." I twisted my hand across the head of his cock and smiled at the hiss of air he let out. "You took care of me last night. It's my turn. Let me take care of you."

His eyes looked nearly black and his grip on my hair tightened. "I'm not going to last long."

"Good." I smiled at him. "Then you won't be late for work."

I flexed my fingers and he swore.

"Come on, baby." I felt his cock pulsing under my hand. He was definitely close. "You're almost there."

"Shae."

My name came out as a moan, and my stomach twisted at the sound.

"I want to watch you come. Come for me, Jas." I didn't want to look away, didn't want to blink. I wanted to see his face when he finally came, to know that I was responsible for making him feel that way.

Suddenly, he groaned, his hips jerking, and hot liquid spilled over my hand. His head tipped back, eyes squeezing closed as he came. He called out my name as I continued to work my hand over his throbbing shaft, milking every last drop until my hand and his stomach were coated with the sticky mess. Only then did I release him.

My day was already off to a better start than yesterday. I just hoped it continued to be that way.

Considering I had to go talk to my favorite detectives today, I doubted it.

***

I'd dressed carefully for my 'interview' today. A black skirt and a nice blouse that would've been appropriate for work, but weren't too dressy for just coming into the station. I wanted to look like I could be on my way to work, but that I could also just have dressed this way to come in and talk. I wasn't planning on lying to the cops if they asked about my job, but I wasn't going to offer the information either. It wasn't any of their business that I'd been suspended. Hell, it was their fault. Them and their stubborn insistence that I must have been involved in Allen's death.

I didn't want them to completely overlook me, since that would mean they were doing their job correctly and considering all possibilities, but I did want them to get their heads out of their asses long enough to realize that I didn't deserve to be the main focus of their attention.

I paused a moment by my car to smooth down my neat, black pencil skirt and then patted my hair to make sure nothing was out of place. I wanted to look calm and collected, but not cold. It was a good thing I'd had at least a couple years teaching under my belt. It helped me maintain that balance between professional and cordial that working with kids required. I couldn't keep myself too distant from my students, or they'd think I didn't care, but too friendly was inappropriate. Teaching had also given me practice in keeping my emotions from showing too much on my face. Especially when working with elementary students, a teacher couldn't let their personal life affect how they treated their students.

I'd just have to think of Detectives Reed and Rheingard as second graders. At least, I thought wryly, it wouldn't be that difficult with Detective Reed. He didn't appear to be the most evolved person I'd met.

I went inside and walked straight past the desk sergeant. I knew where I was going. Both detectives were already at their desks. Reed was nursing a cup of coffee while Rheingard looked busy with some paperwork. I wondered if any of it had to do with me.

"Good morning, Detectives." I kept my voice pleasant, as if the last time I'd seen them, they hadn't been accusing me of homicide.

"Mrs. Lockwood." Detective Rheingard looked up, raising an eyebrow. "We weren't expecting you so early."

"Since I had to cancel yesterday, I figured I should come in early today."

"Feeling any better?"

I turned from Rheingard to Reed and suppressed a scowl. The expression on his face clearly said that he didn't believe that I'd been sick. While that hadn't technically been true, at least in a physical sense, I hadn't been emotionally capable of talking to them last night. That counted as sick, at least in my book.

"Better enough," I said. "Should I take a seat?" I gestured towards the chair next to Reed's desk. I knew we'd end up in an interrogation room again, but I figured it couldn't hurt to try. I was, after all, in here voluntarily.

"Why don't we go somewhere a little more private?" Rheingard suggested, pushing back from his desk.

"You should remember the way." Reed smirked at me as he stood.

I didn't bother to respond. I'd figured out their interrogation strategy before, though I did wonder if

Reed's ignorance and statements intended to provoke were intentional or just part of his obnoxious personality.

"Please have a seat, Mrs. Lockwood." Rheingard held the door open for me to go inside.

I settled in the same chair I sat in before and folded my hands on the table in front of me. Reed and Rheingard sat down, the latter across from me.

"With your permission, Mrs. Lockwood, I'd like to record our interview." Rheingard put a small recorder on the table between us. His eyes cut towards his partner, and then back to me. "Just so there aren't any misunderstandings later."

"Of course," I said amicably. "I don't have anything to hide."

I wondered if Henley had anything to do with that, or if it had come from the DA due to the less-than-honest way the detectives had gone about getting my arrest warrant. I was sure the police department didn't want to risk something like that happening again.

Detective Rheingard pressed the button to record, waited a moment, and then spoke, "First, I want to make it clear that you're not under arrest."

I had a feeling Reed would've liked to have added 'yet' to the end of that statement.

"I understand," I said. "I came in voluntarily to answer any additional questions you might have."

"And we appreciate you having come," Rheingard said.

"Especially since you have such a busy schedule," Reed added. "What with school, and running the vineyard, and your new live-in boyfriend."

I wanted to shake my head in amazement. He was jumping right in there.

"I am busy," I said calmly. "With the holidays coming up and everything, but this is more important. I want to make sure everything possible is done to find out exactly what happened to my late husband."

"Except you know what happened, Mrs. Lockwood," Reed said. He gave me one of those smiles that made me itch to reach across the table and slap him. "But we're going to hold off on that for a moment. We have a couple other matters to discuss before we have you go over the details of that day."

Again, I wanted to add. Go over the details again.

I'd told it so many times that I wasn't even sure how many times I'd said the words anymore.

"You were originally supposed to come in last night after work," Rheingard said.

"I was," I agreed.

"Why didn't you?" he asked.

"I wasn't feeling well," I said. "So I called to reschedule."

"That's not entirely accurate, is it, Mrs. Lockwood?" Detective Rheingard gave me a hard look. "You weren't sick yesterday. You didn't want to come in because you'd been suspended from your job, and you were worried that you'd be too emotional to hide the truth from us."

My fingertips turned white as I pressed them together. How had they known I'd been suspended? Then again, I couldn't say I was entirely surprised. The other teachers would've known, of course, and the office staff. Gossip could spread like wildfire, especially when it was bad.

"I wasn't feeling well," I repeated. "And, yes, a lot of that was due to having been suspended from my job."

"So you lost your job and that made you feel sick so you couldn't come in and answer questions about something you said was important to you?" Reed asked.

"I didn't lose my job," I said tersely. "I was suspended pending the conclusion of this investigation."

"Were you suspended because your employer believes that you might've had something to do with your husband's death?" Rheingard asked.

"No." I put my hands on my lap so the detectives couldn't see me digging my nails into my palms. I had no doubt they'd think it was guilt rather than annoyance.

"Then what was it, Mrs. Lockwood?" Rheingard pressed. "If you don't have anything to hide…"

"The principal is concerned the students might be confused since news of my arrest and the charges were made public." I kept it simple.

"Isn't it true, Mrs. Lockwood, that the real reason you were suspended is because Principal Sanders is afraid for the safety of his students? That he considers you dangerous."

"No," I said, nearly shouting. I took a deep breath before continuing. "I mean..." Shit. "Yes, he's worried about their safety, but not because he thinks *I'd* hurt them. When Aime Vargas came after me, she came into my classroom. He just doesn't want to risk anything happening to the kids." I lifted my chin. "And neither do I."

"So you agree that you should be kept away from your students." Rheingard made it a statement.

"I'm not contesting the suspension," I said. "Doing that would cause more harm than good, and I care about my kids."

"You didn't answer my question," Rheingard said.

"No." I met his gaze and held it. "I don't think I need to be kept away from my students. I don't believe I'm putting them in danger. But I do believe that everything that's going on could be confusing for them."

There was a moment of silence where Rheingard jotted something down in his notebook. I didn't see the point of writing something down when there was a recording of the exact same thing here, but I wasn't a cop. Maybe he was writing down something about my body language. Or maybe it was his lunch order. Who knew.

"Are you aware, Mrs. Lockwood, that your in-laws believe you had something to do with your husband's death?" Detective Rheingard asked.

No shit, Sherlock. I resisted the urge to roll my eyes. I'd been the one who'd told them that the Lockwoods were coming after me.

I kept my answer brief. "Yes, I'm aware."

"They've brought some rather interesting things to our attention," Detective Reed said.

"I'm sure they did." My voice was dry. I couldn't wait to hear this.

Reed leaned across the table towards me and paused a long minute before asking, "How long ago did you and your lover start conspiring to murder your husband?"

Chapter 11

Jasper.

They thought Jasper and I had planned to kill Allen.

The very idea was ludicrous.

Until I remembered that the file and the documents I'd brought to them incriminated Jasper in Allen's death. And since Jasper and I were living together...

Shit.

"Jasper and I didn't kill Allen." I kept my voice as steady and calm as I could make it.

"Right." Reed leaned back in his chair and folded his arms across his chest. "Your husband just happened to die, and a few months later, his best friend moved into your house."

I set my jaw and lifted my chin. I wasn't going to rise to take the bait. Jasper and I had done nothing wrong.

"Let's talk about that insurance money, Mrs. Lockwood," Rheingard spoke. "According to our sources, you claim you didn't know about the insurance until you received a call from them, is that right?"

I nodded. I wasn't even going to ask who their source was. It didn't matter.

"Allen and I had taken out small policies on each other, just enough to cover funeral expenses no matter what our finances would be like at the time of our deaths. That was the only insurance I knew of until I got a call that Allen had taken out a million dollar insurance policy on himself."

"You had your attorney, Mr. Henley, hold the check for you?" Rheingard continued.

"Yes. I wasn't sure what I was going to do with the money, so I asked Mr. Henley to hold it for me until I did."

"But you've since decided that you wanted the money," Reed put in. "Or rather, you wanted to give it to your lover."

My mouth tightened and my nails dug so deeply into my palms that I knew I was going to have marks. "I decided that I was going to give the money to a charity or something like that. I wanted my former in-laws to see that I didn't care about the money."

"But you didn't give the money to a charity. You gave it to the man you were sleeping with."

I had a feeling Reed would've used a much less genteel term if the recorder hadn't been sitting in front of me.

"Allen left Jasper a million dollars from his trust to start a clinic, something that Allen and I both knew Jasper wanted. With Allen's family contesting the will regarding the distribution of the trust, I didn't know how long that money would be tied up.

90

So, yes, I gave Jasper the insurance money so he could start his clinic."

Rheingard made another one of those notes on his notepad. "Your attorney will confirm the dispensation of the insurance policy?"

"Yes. I'll make sure he knows to give you anything you need." I glanced at Reed and saw the skeptical look the detective was giving me. "He can also let you know what's going on with the Lockwoods in regards to Allen's estate. If they haven't already told you everything."

"Speaking of your in-laws," Rheingard said.

I swallowed a sigh. I didn't want to talk about Allen's family, but I wasn't going to protest. I'd answer whatever questions they wanted to ask. I wouldn't give them any reason to think I was holding back.

"We understand that you spoke with your in-laws regarding a DNA sample for a paternity test." Rheingard looked up from his notes.

"I did." I wasn't entirely sure what this had to do with their accusations, but I was willing to go along with it.

As long as they didn't ask where I'd eventually gotten the sample. That wouldn't end well for either Jasper or myself. I was starting to think maybe I should have asked Mr. Henley to come with me.

"Why didn't you have anything in your house with your husband's DNA?" Reed asked. "Toothbrush. Hair brushes." He paused and smirked suggestively. "Sheets."

I ignored the not-so-subtle innuendo. "By the

time the paternity suit came around, I'd already cleaned out anything of Allen's that would've had his DNA."

"Right," Reed said. "Because you had to make room for your new lover."

I got the impression he liked using that word. My voice was tight. "Because I'm trying to move on with my life. Like my husband would have wanted."

Reed sneered. "I'm sure he would've been ecstatic about you...living with his friend."

I had to bite my tongue from snapping at him. Defending my relationship with Jasper wasn't what was needed at the moment.

"You'd gotten rid of all of Allen's things?" Rheingard asked.

"No," I clarified. "I'd thrown away things like his toothbrush and hairbrush. His razor. Things that couldn't be donated or that I wasn't going to keep. So, no, I haven't thrown away everything that belonged to my husband. I just didn't have anything I could use for the test."

Rheingard raised an eyebrow. "And what does Dr. Whitehall think about the fact that you still have some of your husband's things at the house?"

"Allen was Jasper's best friend." I met his eyes and worked to keep my voice steady. "He misses my late husband as much as I do. There's no competition between them."

Reed didn't even try to hide his skepticism. "Seems to me you'd have to be a pretty cold-hearted bit–," he cleared his throat, "person to sleep with your husband's best friend."

"Did you know Allen? Either of you?" I asked suddenly. "Do you know Jasper? I mean, beyond a professional capacity or rumors?"

The men exchanged glances before Rheingard answered, "No. We never met Mr. Lockwood, and our encounters with Dr. Whitehall have been brief."

"Then I don't really think either of you are qualified to tell me what my late husband or my current lover," I looked at Reed when I used the word, "would think about me or this situation." I gave them both a humorless smile. "So why don't we stick to the relevant questions? That's what I'm here to answer, after all."

A moment of silence followed my little speech, and then Detective Reed heaved out a sigh and pushed his chair back.

"I need coffee."

He disappeared through the door, leaving me with Detective Rheingard.

"Can I get you anything to drink?"

I shook my head. "I just want to get this over with, Detective."

He nodded. "All right. Why don't you tell me again about what happened that day?" He gestured towards the recorder. "We'll get it on tape this time."

I doubted that had anything to do with why he was asking me to repeat the same things I'd already told him a dozen times in a dozen ways. But I did it one more time. I barely even had to think about what I was saying as I went through it all again.

By the time I finished, Detective Reed had returned with his coffee. I didn't even pause when he slumped down in his chair and glared at me, sipping at his drink.

When I finished, Rheingard did his little note-taking thing, and then looked over at Detective Reed.

I could almost hear them saying *tag, you're it*.

"When did you choke your husband?" Reed asked.

I stared at him, mouth hanging open. "When did I what?"

"Choke him," Reed repeated. He straightened and leaned forward. "Or did you hit him? The medical examiner couldn't get a clear picture of what happened before you managed to get your husband's body removed."

"What are you talking about?" I wasn't even annoyed with the question because I had no clue what he was talking about. "Allen died because his parachute didn't open."

"Right," Reed agreed. His eyes were gleaming. "But the medical examiner made a note of a suspicious-looking bruise on Allen's neck."

"How could they...I mean, he was..." The words stuck in my throat. I might've been moving on and putting my life together again, but that didn't make it any easier to think about what happened that day. Especially not about how Allen had died.

"Detective." Rheingard's voice was sharp. He looked over at his partner and then turned back to me. "The medical examiner didn't report a bruise."

I glared at Detective Reed. It figured the asshole was lying to me again to try to get me to say I'd done something I hadn't done. He'd been trying to get me worked up over the brutality of Allen's death so I'd say something incriminating. I'd known he was a heartless bastard, but that was beyond cold.

Rheingard continued, "We do, however, have a statement from one of the men who worked at the airfield that says Mr. Lockwood had a strange-looking bruise on his neck."

I gave him a confused look. "I don't understand."

"Is it possible that something may have happened before you got on the plane? Something that may have caused Mr. Lockwood to pass out?"

I was thoroughly confused now. Were both detectives lying to me about the bruise? Were they trying to trick me into saying that Allen and I'd had some sort of fight before he died? Like that would've given some sort of reason to kill him? Was Rheingard giving me a different sort of lie after calling Reed out because what he did was supposed to make me think he was telling the truth?

"You and Mr. Lockwood didn't have any sort of altercation? An argument that maybe got a little out of hand?" Rheingard pressed.

"No!" I snapped. "If you must know, Allen and I had spent the night before and the morning of the accident having sex. We weren't fighting. We were fucking."

Rheingard at least had the decency to look slightly embarrassed by my blunt wording, but Reed just sat there with that stupid smirk on his face.

And then it hit me and my face flushed.

95

Shit.

I knew what he was talking about.

"The, um, bruise," I started. "Was it here?" I pointed to a place on my own neck.

"Yes." Rheingard nodded.

"Yeah, um..." My ears were burning. "I did do that."

"So you're admitting that you put a bruise on your husband's throat before you got into the airplane?" Rheingard glanced at his partner. "If it somehow caused Mr. Lockwood to pass out and forget to open his parachute, it wasn't intentional..."

"It wasn't a bruise," I interrupted. "It was a hickey."

If I'd known that such a statement would effectively shut them both up for nearly a full minute, I might've said it sooner.

Then Detective Reed opened his mouth and I knew whatever he was going to say would be rude.

"Yes, Detective Reed," I spoke before he could. "I gave my husband a hickey when we were making love on our anniversary. He gave me one too. I doubt either of them caused my husband's parachute to not open, but I do know my sex life isn't any of your business."

Another moment of uncomfortable silence followed before Detective Rheingard spoke, "The thing is, your sex life is our business. Especially when it comes to this investigation."

"What the hell does my sex life have to do with this, other than the fact that it explains the mark on Allen's neck?"

Detective Reed put his elbows on the table and laced his fingers together. "You didn't answer our original question, Mrs. Lockwood. How long had you and Dr. Whitehall been having an affair before the two of you decided to kill your husband?"

I closed my eyes and shook my head. "You know what? I've had enough of this. I came in to answer legitimate questions, but all you keep doing is going over the same stuff I've already answered, and being rude to me." I stood up. "I'm done here. If you want to speak to me again, call my lawyer. He'll come in with me because I'm tired of this. Good day, detectives."

Chapter 12

I called Mr. Henley as soon as I came out of the police station. I knew the detectives were furious, and Henley wasn't going to like it either, so I figured it was better that he hear it from me.

I explained things to him as quickly as I could, not wanting to give him a chance to comment until I was done. When I did finally fall silent, his reaction was exactly what I expected.

"Shae." He gave a heavy sigh. "That was probably not the best thing you could've done."

"I know," I admitted. "But I just couldn't take any more of it. All they have is a bunch of suspicions without any proof and they're wasting all their time on questioning me when they should be accepting that Allen did it to himself. There's proof of that right in the letter I gave them."

"You do know if they rule it a suicide, the insurance company is going to want their money back," Henley said. "In fact, I'm surprised they released it at all. They usually wait for a ruling, but what's done is done. Even if someone jumped the gun in sending you the check, you won't be allowed to keep it if the detectives officially rule it suicide."

"I know," I said. "And I don't care. I just want this to be done so that I can try to have a normal life again."

"Well, I'll do whatever I can to make that possible." There was a pause, and then he spoke again, "Are you heading into work now?"

Right. He didn't know.

"Not exactly."

"Can you come by my office? There are a couple new developments I'd like to discuss."

That was probably a good thing since I had to explain my suspension. I just hoped what he had to say made up for my plethora of bad news.

***

By the time I was on my way home, I was ready to chalk up the day as a complete loss.

The events at the police station had been awful, making me re-live seeing Allen die, hearing the accusations about Jasper and myself. They made what Jasper and I had into something sordid, the sort of thing the people of St. Helena had been gossiping about. That hurt me almost as much as the rest.

My meeting with Mr. Henley hadn't been much better, and the information he'd given me continued to circle in my mind. It was heading towards late afternoon by the time I pulled into the driveway and I already felt like my brain was going to explode.

I didn't even register that Jasper's car was in the driveway until I opened the door and smelled something wonderful. He was home.

"Jas?" I called his name as I stepped inside.

"Hey, babe." He stepped out of the kitchen, a smile lighting up his face when he saw me.

"Why aren't you at work?" I asked as he came towards me.

"Left early," he said, wrapping his arms around me. He bent his head and gave me a brief, but intense kiss. "I thought you might have a rough day, and since I wasn't here last night when you needed me because I was at work, I figured work could take the back seat today."

It was on the tip of my tongue to say that it hadn't been work that needed him last night, but rather Georgia. I didn't though. It would've sounded petty because it would've been petty. I didn't like the woman or how she behaved with Jasper, but he was mine, so she wasn't even close to the top of my problems list.

"I'm glad you're here." I pressed my face against his chest, closing my eyes as I breathed in his scent. "Saying it was a rough day is an understatement."

"What happened, love?" He ran his hand over my hair.

I shook my head. "What smells so good?" I smiled. "Besides you."

He chuckled, the rumble a gentle sound in my ear. "I'm making dinner. Roasted chicken with cooked carrots. Fresh Asiago bread from Augustine's Bakery and a blueberry pie ready to go in the oven when the chicken comes out."

I groaned, mouth watering at the thought of all that wonderful food. "You are amazing."

"I like to think so." He wrapped his arm around

101

my shoulders, and used his other hand to take my purse. "We still have some time before the chicken's done. Why don't you go sit on the couch, and I'll bring you something to drink. You want beer or wine?"

I smiled, loving that he asked and didn't assume. "How about a beer before dinner and wine with it?"

He grinned. "Sounds good."

He headed back into the kitchen while I kicked off my dress shoes and went into the living room. I settled on the couch, pulling my feet up under me as I closed my eyes and rested my head on the back of the couch.

I felt the couch shift as Jasper sat next to me and I turned my head, opening my eyes to look at him. He held out a bottle of beer and I took it gratefully. As I took a long drink, he reached down to pick up my feet. I shifted with him so that my feet were on his lap. He reached under my skirt to pull down one stocking, then the other, leaving my feet bare.

He didn't ask any questions or even try to make small talk. He just took my foot in his hands and began to work his thumbs against the sole of my foot.

"Fuck," I breathed. My eyelids fluttered. "That feels amazing."

He smiled and kept rubbing, his thumbs finding all of the right spots that reached places inside me that touching a foot shouldn't be able to reach. I felt myself beginning to relax. When he started on my other foot, I was okay enough to tell him what had happened at the police station.

He was silent through all of it, only the tension I could sense in his body told me what he was feeling. When I got to the part about Detective Reed asking how long our affair had been going on, he swore softly.

"That was the last straw," I said. "All of the accusations were awful, but I couldn't stand them acting like we'd done something wrong, like our relationship was something I needed to be ashamed of."

"What did you say?" he asked as his thumbs moved up to the muscle right under my big toe.

"I told them I was done, and if they wanted to talk to me again, to call my attorney because I wasn't going to put up with their behavior." I took another drink of my beer. "Then I walked out and called Mr. Henley to tell him what I'd done."

"What did he have to say?"

I shrugged. "Pretty much what I expected. That what I'd done hadn't been the best idea, but then he asked me to come to his office because he had some new information he wanted to share in person."

I drained the last of my beer and set the empty bottle on the coffee table. I could feel the edges of everything start to turn fuzzy. It wasn't enough that I forgot about my problems, but the alcohol had definitely helped. That and a glass of wine with dinner and I'd be pleasantly buzzed all night.

"What did Mr. Henley have to tell you?" Jasper asked, his fingers switching from massaging to running over my ankles and the tops of my feet. The touch was light enough to be just this side of ticklish, and it sent shivers of pleasure across my nerves.

"He's convinced that everything the cops have is circumstantial, easily explained away, but that he's seen cases where circumstantial evidence, when put together in a believable story, end up in a conviction."

"You're innocent," Jasper said. "No one in their right mind would think you killed Allen."

I raised an eyebrow at him. "Seriously? You think a jury would look at me and think that I didn't care about the inheritance? That I just happened to fall in love with my husband's best friend only a couple of months after the accident?"

"It won't get that far," he said firmly. "They tried arresting you once and a judge threw it out."

"But a judge signed off on it in the first place," I countered. "And, granted, the detectives hadn't exactly been honest with what they'd told her they had on me, but if they put together a strong circumstantial case, there's always a possibility someone will listen." I sighed. "And that's even without the Lockwoods getting involved."

"What did they do now?" Jasper asked, his eyes darkening into that stormy sort of gray that came when he was upset.

"We don't have any proof," I said. "But Mr. Henley has been talking to some friends of his in the DA's office and there are rumors going around that some of the people higher up are pushing things forward. Like the judge who signed the original arrest warrant hadn't been quite as thorough or careful as she ought to have been."

"You don't think the Lockwoods are actually bribing anyone, do you?" Jasper asked. "I mean, I'm not so sure they wouldn't be capable of it, but those would be some serious accusations."

I shrugged. "I don't know, Jas. When Allen was alive, I would've said no way. They might have been willing to lie to get what they wanted, but I never would've thought they'd cross into anything blatantly illegal. Even some of the stuff they pulled about Allen's will wasn't exactly surprising."

"And now?"

"They set fire to the vineyard." I frowned. "Or at least hired someone to do it. Even if they're never charged for it, you and I both know they're responsible. That was crossing a line I never wanted to think they'd cross."

"What did Henley say you should do?"

I sighed. "Well, there's not really much of anything I can do right now except wait. The detectives will either take what they have, and use it to exonerate or charge me, or they'll called Henley to set up another interview with me." I gave him a serious look. "And you might want to consider looking into a lawyer for yourself. I have a feeling they might be coming for you next."

He shrugged. "We'll deal with that when the time comes. Right now, I'm more worried about you. What did Mr. Henley say about the Lockwoods?"

"He said he'll try to dig a little deeper, but neither of us think he'll be able to find anything. They're too used to hiding stuff like this back in Texas. They can cover their tracks."

"Does he think you're going to be charged again?"

"He didn't say it, but I think I will. Those detectives aren't going to let this go, especially not if they have higher ups encouraging them."

Jasper was quiet for a moment, and then his fingers tightened around my ankle. I raised my head to look at him.

"What do you need from me?"

"I need to not think," I said. "I need all of the chaos in my head to quiet down, at least for a while, or I'm going to go crazy."

He gave me a smile, the kind of smile that warmed everything inside me. "I think I can manage that."

Chapter 13

I started to sit up, desire pooling in my belly, but Jasper shook his head.

"The bedroom?" I started to ask.

"I want you here." His voice was low as he wrapped his hands around my ankles and gave me a tug so that I was half-laying on the couch. His eyes danced with humor as he added, "I need to be able to hear the oven timer. Don't want to burn dinner."

I rolled my eyes, a smile curving my lips as he crawled up my body until we were face to face. He held himself over me until our bodies were barely touching, but it didn't matter. Electricity buzzed between us, filling the air until I could barely breathe, and he hadn't even done anything yet.

Still keeping his body above mine, he lowered only his face so that he could brush his lips across mine. His tongue darted out, teasing my mouth until I chased it back, turning a light touch into a full kiss. I put my hands on the back of his neck and yanked him down. I didn't want gentle and sweet.

"Make me forget," I whispered against his mouth before I took his bottom lip between my teeth.

I wrapped my legs around his waist and pulled him towards me. I moaned as he let his weight rest against me. My fingers made their way through his hair as he took control of the kiss, claiming my mouth with the sort of reckless abandon that had caused us to make love out in the vineyard, in the closet of my former in-laws' house. This was what I wanted, something fierce and wild enough to make me not think about anything else.

He tugged at the buttons of my blouse, impatience nearly ripping some free. I didn't care. I just wanted his hands on me. He pushed my bra up as soon as he had my shirt open enough, not bothering to remove either one. His fingers rolled and pinched and pulled on my nipples until I was whimpering against his questing tongue.

He kissed down my neck and across my collarbone before moving down to my breasts. I buried my fingers in his hair, twisting the silky strands between my fingers as he teased me by placing open-mouthed kisses across my breasts, sucking and nipping at the flesh, but never touching my nipples. When he finally closed his lips around one of them, my body jerked, a hiss of satisfaction coming between my teeth.

I closed my eyes and gave myself over to the scorching wet heat. Every pull of his mouth went straight through me, as if he had a direct line from my breast to that throbbing place deep inside me. My panties were soaked by the time he switched from one breast to the other.

He wriggled a hand between us, finding the

button of my pants. As he was working that open, I tugged on his shirt, needing to feel his skin under my hands. I had it bunched by his shoulders when he managed to get his hand into my pants. My nails raked across his back while his fingers slid beneath the waistband of my panties to find me slick and wet.

"Oh, baby." His voice was rough. "I love that I do this to you."

His fingers pressed against my clit and I gasped, my back arching. He took my nipple into his mouth again, sucking hard on the sensitive flesh even as he slid a finger inside me. My eyelids fluttered as he worked his finger into me, my pants keeping his hand pressed tightly to me, putting pressure and the most delicious friction on my clit with every move he made. Between his hand between my legs and his mouth on my breast, I lost myself in the exquisite sensations coursing through me. With his usual single-minded determination, he worked me towards climax until I finally exploded around him.

I was still coming down when he pushed himself up on his knees and began to yank at my pants and underwear, pulling them both down to the middle of my thighs. He flipped me over, easily maneuvering my still-limp body until I was on my knees in front of the couch, my elbows on the seat.

Jasper moved behind me, his hands caressing my bare ass before moving to my hips. I felt his cock nudge against me, and then he was pushing inside. But he was too big and I couldn't spread my legs any further. My head fell forward as he relentlessly worked his way into me, each inch making me gasp and pant as he stretched me.

"Fuck." The word burst out of me. "Fuck. Fuck."

"You are so tight," Jasper ground out. His fingers massaged my hips as he came to rest inside me. He curled his body over mine and pressed his lips to my ear. "Are you okay?"

I nodded. I pushed back against him. "Please."

He slid his hands beneath me, cupping my breasts as he moved. Short, shallow thrusts that deepened as he straightened. My clit throbbed in response to Jasper's fingers manipulating my swollen nipples, each twist and pull sending a jolt of painful pleasure into my system.

My breath came in bursts as he thrust into me, his cock rubbing every inch of me. There were nerves being stroked that I hadn't even been aware of until now, and I shuddered at the first wave of pleasure that washed over me.

"Come for me, baby," Jasper murmured in my ear. "I'm almost there."

One of his hands left my breast and slid down my stomach. The tip of his finger brushed over my clit. I groaned, shivering. I felt his teeth through the fabric of my shirt as he bit down on my shoulder and I moaned. His finger made circles on my clit, each one pushing me closer to another orgasm.

And then I was there, tipping over the edge, calling out his name as I came. He followed a moment later, buried deep inside me. He slumped over my back, his arms wrapped around me, holding me until we both came down. I hissed as he pulled out, suddenly feeling empty. He settled on the floor, pulling me onto his lap so he could kiss me.

He brushed back my hair, resting his forehead on mine. "Dinner should be done soon. Why don't you go get cleaned up, get into something comfortable and by then, we should be ready to eat."

"Thank you," I said. "For distracting me."

He smiled and kissed the tip of my nose. "We're just getting started. I plan on distracting you all night."

***

He made good on his promise.

Dinner was amazing. Everything had been cooked to perfection. The wine was excellent. We made small talk about things that had nothing to do with legal issues or my job or anything important. We talked about how things were going at the clinic, and what we wanted to do for Thanksgiving. When we were done, he cleaned off the table while I finished my wine.

I figured we'd spend the rest of the night watching tv, just enjoying time together. Instead, Jasper held out his hand and led me back to the bedroom. He didn't say a word as he undressed me, taking me out of the yoga pants and sweatshirt I'd put on earlier, his eyes darkening when he saw that I hadn't bothered with new undergarments.

"You are so beautiful." He looked up at me from where he was on his knees. He kissed my hip and I shivered. He smiled as he put his hand on my knee. "Hold on to me."

I put my hand on his shoulder as he lifted my

leg, putting it on his other shoulder. The movement spread me open and, for a moment, I felt a flash of embarrassment, but then I saw the look on Jasper's face and forgot to be embarrassed. He cupped my ass in his hands and leaned forward, pressing his mouth against me.

My head fell forward and I moaned. His tongue danced over my skin, then darted inside, tasting me. I wanted to move, to press myself closer to his mouth, but he held me tight as he continued to lick every inch of me except the one place I desperately wanted him.

Then he was there, tongue and lips focused on that little point of nerves. He teased and sucked until I was crying out, my hands digging into his hair as I came. And even then he didn't let up, driving me from one orgasm into the next, holding me as my legs gave out.

My entire body was limp as he stood and eased me onto the bed. He stripped off his clothes quickly, then stretched out next to me, propping himself up on his elbow. His expression was strangely serious as his fingers traced patterns on my stomach.

"I told you I was going to make you forget about today, take you out of your head." His eyes met mine. "Do you trust me?"

My stomach clenched and I nodded. I may have questioned my faith in him before, may have thought perhaps I'd misjudged him, and that he wasn't the man I knew him to be.

Not anymore. I didn't just love him. I trusted him. And I was going to show him.

"Roll over."

I rolled onto my stomach.

"Spread your legs."

As I did what he asked, I felt his fingers brush against the insides of my thighs, then two slid inside. I moaned, but his fingers weren't there long, only two quick strokes and then his fingers were moving up higher.

"Shit," I breathed as the tip of one finger circled my anus.

"Have you...?"

The question trailed off, but I didn't need him to ask the rest of it. "No." I shook my head.

"You tell me to stop, and I will," he promised.

I nodded to indicate that I understood.

He took it slow, easing his finger into me and working it until the burn eased. When he added a second finger, I closed my eyes, focusing on keeping my breathing even, my muscles relaxed. It was a strange sensation, feeling his fingers moving inside that place, stretching things that had never been stretched before.

When his hand disappeared, I felt the mattress shift as he moved between my legs. I clenched my hands together and waited.

"Just say the word and I'll stop." Jasper's voice was soft. He put his hand on the small of my back. "Relax and let me take care of you."

I nodded again.

Something blunt and much bigger than his fingers pushed against me. I exhaled as my body resisted, then stretched. I made a strangled sound as

113

the head of his cock popped past the ring of muscle and he stilled, one hand on my hip.

"I've got you, love." He slid his hand underneath me, his fingers gently rubbing my clit. "Let me in."

I still had that uncomfortable feeling of fullness, but the pleasurable sensations coming from my clit began to spread out, and I felt my body relax, letting his cock slip further in. He rocked his hips, easing himself deeper even as his fingers continued to rub my clit.

"Almost there, baby," he said. "You're going to feel so good, I promise."

I nodded, not trusting myself to speak. My fingers were curled in the sheets, tears burning my eyes, but I wasn't going to ask him to stop. It wasn't painful exactly, not with his fingers giving me pleasure to merge with the pain. But I was so full. I didn't know if it could actually feel good, but I was going to trust him.

When he was finally all the way inside, he waited, one hand still underneath me, the other running up and down my spine. Finally, he began to move, drawing back, then easing forward. I let out a shuddering breath as he repeated the move. I couldn't say it felt pleasant yet, but the burn had lessened.

I lost track of time as it narrowed down to the sensation of him moving in and out of me, of his fingers keeping constant pressure on my clit. Soon, the pain became something else, something more intense than what I'd felt before. He began to thrust faster, and I could feel the familiar pressure beginning to build.

"I want you to come, baby." His voice was rough. "You think you can come like this?"

If he'd asked me when we'd first begun, I would've told him no. Now, I wasn't so sure.

"Come for me, Shae."

I gasped as he slid a finger into my pussy, his thumb continuing to move over my clit.

"I want to feel you come." He drove in hard enough to make me cry out. "I want you to come. Feel you squeeze my cock, my finger."

He twisted his hand at what had to have been a nearly impossible angle, his knuckle pushing against my g-spot even as he pushed his cock deep into my ass, putting extra pressure on the finger inside me. I shuddered as I hit the edge and then keened as he did it again and I came. He grabbed my hips, driving into me over and over again, overloading me on sensation. And then he was coming, calling my name as he emptied himself into me.

Later that night, after we'd cleaned up and crawled back into bed, I snuggled up to him, resting my head on his chest. He put his arm around me, his fingers making small circles on my upper arm.

"Thank you," I said.

"For what?"

I turned my head to kiss his chest. "For doing exactly what you promised. Making me forget."

He was quiet for a moment, then asked, "Did you...like it?"

I raised my head and gave him a questioning look. "Seriously? You did feel me come, right?"

"I wasn't sure..." His voice trailed off as he turned his head away.

"Jas," I said his name gently. "I don't fake it."

He looked down at me, a vulnerable expression on his face. "It's just...I don't want you to think I only...I mean..."

"Jas." I pushed myself up and kissed him. "If I hadn't wanted to do it, I would've said so. Did it hurt? A bit. Was it worth it? Yes." I settled back down on his chest. "I love you."

His arm tightened around me. "I love you too."

Chapter 14

Since I didn't have to worry about work for a while, or even grading papers over the holiday, I decided to spend the Wednesday before Thanksgiving focused on making my first real holiday without Allen more than just bearable. I knew I'd been fortunate in the timing of Allen's death when it came to holidays. I'd had some time to heal. I knew there would be things about the holidays that would make me sad, but it wasn't going to ruin them.

Jasper and I talked it over and decided we wanted to do a small Thanksgiving here. I called Mitchell first thing this morning to invite him to come, but he'd told me he'd been seeing someone for a few weeks and she'd invited him to spend Thanksgiving with her family. Since he'd never mentioned that he'd been dating someone, I suspected he'd made it up to have an excuse for not having to spend the day pretending that things weren't strained between the three of us. I didn't call him on it though. There was always the chance he just hadn't told me about his new girlfriend.

While I loved my brother, I had to admit that I

felt some relief that he wouldn't be there. I had so much else going on, so much I needed to deal with, having Mitchell there would just be one more thing on my mind. The last thing I wanted to do was spend all of Thanksgiving wondering if Mitchell was going to make some ignorant comment to or about me and Jasper.

Jasper hadn't even considered going to his parents' house. When I'd asked him about it, he'd simply said that when he'd quit working at his father's practice, his father had made it perfectly clear that Jasper's decision was the same as choosing me over his family. Knowing that Jasper's relationship with his family was rocky, I hadn't pressed the matter.

Instead of worrying about our families or any of the other stuff going on in our lives, I focused on getting the house ready for the next day and planning the menu. I'd planned half a dozen Thanksgiving meals for Allen, Jasper, Mitchell and myself, but I wanted this one to be different. I didn't want Jasper to feel like he was a replacement for Allen by keeping everything else the same.

I didn't decorate as much as I had in the past, but I did get into one of the closets to get out a few things. While Jasper was in at the clinic, I put out the decorations and got to work cleaning. I scrubbed the place from top to bottom, letting myself get lost in the physical activity of it. By the time I was done and showered, my entire body was aching. Adding in how sore certain parts of my anatomy were from the previous night, I was glad I had leftovers from what

Jasper had made yesterday so I didn't have to cook anything else.

Jasper and I kept it casual, eating in the living room while we watched the news. While I'd thoroughly enjoyed how we'd spent the night before, I was glad for some down time where all we were doing was sitting on the couch, holding hands, leaning on each other. Sitting like this, planning what we wanted to eat tomorrow, what we were going to do, made me feel almost normal.

We woke late for us the next morning, but still early enough to enjoy the parade while we ate the cinnamon rolls I'd bought specifically for today. After breakfast, we put on a football game in the background even though neither of us were particularly interested in either team playing. Jasper was a Colts fan and this hadn't been their year. I could pretty much take or leave the game. Still, football and Thanksgiving went hand-in-hand.

The turkey went into the bottom oven so it'd be ready late afternoon. The top was reserved for switching between toasting the bread and baking the pre-made pumpkin pies I'd bought. We went back and forth between the kitchen and the living room, checking on food, commenting on the score or various plays.

When everything was ready, we headed into the dining room to eat. The food turned out amazing and we spent the first few minutes in silence, simply enjoying the meal.

"You know, the only good holidays I had were the ones I had with you and Allen." He took another sip of his wine. "Holidays with you two were the only ones where I knew I didn't have to worry about who was going to say what, or pretend to be someone I wasn't."

I reached over and put my hand over his. He flipped his over, and threaded his fingers through mine.

"I don't have any good memories of holidays with my family," he said quietly. "Not one. Not even before I pulled all that shit as a teenager and they had an excuse to treat..." His voice trailed off.

My heart ached for him, for the child he'd been. I'd known only bits and pieces about his childhood, enough to know that it hadn't been a happy one. His parents seemed to be those kinds of people who wanted the world to think they had the perfect family, and anyone who didn't fit that mold didn't belong.

"Thank you for doing this today. I know it couldn't have been easy for you." His fingers tightened around mine.

"I miss him," I said honestly. "But it's different than how it was. It's not so much that I wish he was here because I can't be happy without him, but I do miss him."

"I do too." He raised our hands and brushed his lips across my knuckles. "I know exactly what you mean. I love you and I know if he was here, we wouldn't be together, but a part of me still wishes he was here."

I wanted to reassure him, to tell him that if Allen hadn't died, we still would've ended up together, but

I couldn't say it. Allen's death had changed me, and it was that change that had brought Jasper and I together. If Allen was still alive, I wouldn't be me, not this me. And I would still have loved him.

"It messes with my head sometimes," Jasper admitted. "Like how I can wish Allen wasn't dead, when I know that if he was still alive, I wouldn't have you? But how can I be happy I have you, without being happy Allen's dead?"

"I get it," I said. "It's hard to separate everything."

He nodded. "And that's always going to be there, isn't it?"

"I think so," I said.

He was quiet for a moment, thoughtful. "How do you deal with it?"

We'd talked about Allen, shared memories of our times together. We'd both talked about how Allen would've wanted us to be happy and would have wanted me to love again. We hadn't talked about this though. We hadn't objectively discussed how we each balanced missing Allen with our new happiness. Because I was happy, despite all of the other stuff going on around me. Jasper made me happy, made me feel safe.

I shrugged. "I admit I can never reconcile those two things. I loved Allen and I miss him, but I love you and I'm happy with you."

He gave me a soft smile. "I love you too."

After a moment, I turned back to my plate. "Do you have anything that you normally do the day after Thanksgiving? Black Friday shopping?"

He shook his head. "I always just worked, even if it was volunteering at the ER."

"You worked a lot over the holidays," I said, remembering.

"I never had any reason not to," he said. "I liked to let other people spend the holidays with their families since I never wanted to be with mine, and I only had a couple hours with you and Allen."

"Well, you have a family to be with now," I said. "So no working Christmas Eve or Christmas Day."

"Agreed." He smiled. "Do you want me to close the clinic tomorrow? We could stay home and decorate for Christmas."

My stomach tightened as I thought of decorating the house for my favorite holiday. Allen and I always did that together the day after Thanksgiving. We'd spend the night before watching movies together, and then we'd sleep late the next day. After breakfast, we'd take down the fall decorations, and then start putting up the Christmas ones...

"Did I say something wrong?" Jasper's voice was concerned.

"No." I shook my head. "Sorry. I was just thinking about how Allen and I used to decorate the day after Thanksgiving..."

"We don't have to," Jasper said quickly. "Whatever you want. We can decorate a different day, or you can do it whenever. A bit at a time."

"I don't know," I said. "I'm just not sure if I can handle a big Christmas. I mean, I want to do Christmas. With you. But I don't know if I can do all of the things...I mean, decorating, and hosting a party and..."

"Hey." He leaned forward and pressed his lips firmly against mine. "We don't have to do any of that. Even if it's just you and me exchanging gifts Christmas morning, that's enough." He smiled. "Hell, we don't even have to do that. I just want to be able to wake up next to you and know that I finally get to spend Christmas morning with the person I love."

I smiled back, grateful for his understanding. I wanted to give him a wonderful Christmas, just like we were having a great Thanksgiving. I didn't know if I'd be able to do it, but for Jasper, I was willing to try.

Chapter 15

Part of me was glad that Jasper had decided to work the day after Thanksgiving. More of me was glad that he decided to go in late because he woke me up with one orgasm and then fucked me into another. All in all, it was a great way to wake up and I couldn't deny that I'd thoroughly enjoyed watching him getting dressed after. I liked him getting undressed even more, but I wasn't going to ask him to spend the day in bed, no matter how tempting it was.

After he left, I got up and spent the rest of the day cleaning up from yesterday. We had plenty of leftovers so I nibbled as I packed it up in separate containers, each one enough for a meal. We'd be good through the whole weekend. I'd gone a bit overboard with the food, but it wouldn't have felt like Thanksgiving otherwise.

It was strange, taking down the fall decorations and not putting up the Christmas ones I knew were sitting in boxes upstairs. A part of me still wanted to go up and get the decorations, put them all in their usual places. I wanted to stand in the living room and see the place where the tree would go, see the stockings hanging up...

Shit. I sat down on the edge of the couch. I couldn't do it. I couldn't put up the decorations Allen and I had bought together. I couldn't put up my stocking without seeing his matching one, even if it was only in my imagination. And the tree. We'd gotten a fake plastic one our first year together and even though it had been a fairly cheap one, we'd kept it. And then there were the ornaments. Some of them were ones I'd gotten as a child and teenager, but a lot were ones that Allen and I had bought together. I didn't think I could look at those either. Not today at least.

While I didn't get any decorating done, I did manage to put a dent in my Christmas shopping online. Not that I had a lot of people to buy for anymore, I suddenly realized. There was Mitchell and Jasper, of course. Mitchell's girlfriend if she really existed and still existed at Christmastime. But unless the two of us happened to become best friends before then, the best I could do for her would be something vague and impersonal. I'd be buying something for Gina and Junie too. I usually bought something small for Principal Sanders and did a fruit tray for all of the teachers, but if I wasn't back to work by then, I wasn't about to go out of my way to buy anything for them.

And I didn't have to buy for the Lockwoods. Or, more accurately, attempt to buy for them. Every year that I'd been with Allen, I'd tried to buy Christmas presents for Allen's parents, both of his siblings, their spouses, and their kids. And every year, they

126

smiled and pretended to love whatever it was I'd given them. Then I'd hear them making comments to each other as if I couldn't hear them. Reasons why what I'd bought hadn't been good enough, or had been the wrong thing altogether. All of the excuses they'd use to justify exchanging, or simply returning, whatever it was I'd gotten them.

For the first time since before I'd met Allen, there was a good possibility that all of my gifts would actually be kept.

It was surprising how relieved I was by that.

***

When I got up Monday morning, Jasper was already gone, but he'd left me a note on the refrigerator.

Miss you. Love you. - J

Four words, one letter. And my insides were all mush.

I traced his initial with my finger and smiled. Maybe tonight we could talk about some things we could do for Christmas that wouldn't involve getting into memories. Some new things that we could make our own.

Someone knocked on the door. I frowned. I'd told Jacques to take off today and tomorrow too. He'd done so much for me.

When I opened the door, however, it wasn't Jacques on the other side. It was Detectives Reed and Rheingard.

"Can I help you?" I managed to give them a polite smile.

"Mrs. Lockwood." Detective Reed held out a

piece of paper. "We have a search warrant for your house."

I took the paper, staring at it as a string of cops stepped past me and into the house. A search warrant? Why were they searching my house? What were they looking for?

"Mrs. Lockwood." Detective Rheingard stepped closer and looked down at me. "You'll want to set that down."

"Why?" My head was reeling.

The detectives exchanged a look and I set down the warrant. I didn't want to think it, but I knew where this was going.

Again.

"Shae Lockwood, you're under arrest..."

I let the words wash over me as I heard them for the second time. It felt even more surreal than before. Here I was, in my comfy yoga pants and sweatshirt, getting my hands cuffed behind my back and I almost couldn't believe it was happening. There were men in my house, going through my things, trying to find something to prove that I'd killed Allen. And I was being arrested again.

I decided that this time, I would play things differently. I'd tried doing what I thought was the right thing before. I'd talked to them without a lawyer, thinking that would prove that I was innocent. I'd answered their questions over and over. I hadn't lied about anything. I'd even taken them a personal letter because I'd thought it would help.

Fuck that.

This time, I was exercising my right to remain silent. I didn't say a word during the drive back to the station or even when they walked me inside. They went through the same things they'd done before when they'd booked me, Reed running his mouth the entire time. Since I hadn't asked for a lawyer, I knew he was trying to get me to say something incriminating that could be admitted into evidence. Even though I didn't really have anything that could incriminate me because I was innocent, I wasn't going to give him the satisfaction of knowing that he'd managed to get under my skin enough to make me talk about anything.

By the time I was finally put into an interrogation room, it was all I could do to keep my temper. Even Rheingard seemed annoyed with how far Reed had taken things. His insinuations about Jasper and my relationship had gone from not-so-subtle innuendos to flat-out filth. The one reaction I hadn't been able to control was my face and the fact that it was burning was amusing Reed to no end.

The smirk fell off his face the minute I sat down, looked straight at him and said the magic words.

"I want to call my lawyer."

Detective Rheingard simply looked resigned, as if he'd expected me to lawyer up. Detective Reed looked like I'd just stolen his birthday present. He all but stomped out of the room, leaving me alone with Rheingard. I leaned back in my chair and waited.

Mr. Henley arrived less than a half hour after I called him. He rather politely asked the detective to leave us alone, and then began to explain what he'd found out.

"This arrest warrant is going to stick," Henley said with a frown. "They don't have any real evidence, but this judge has decided that he's going to let things play out."

"Do you think that the Lockwoods are pushing it?" I asked.

Henley sighed. "I do, but it'd be practically impossible to prove it."

"So what happens next?" I asked. I hadn't expected the Lockwoods to be held accountable for any of that.

"They legally have to get you in front of a judge for arraignment within twenty-four hours."

"I could be here all night." I closed my eyes. I had no doubt that would be the case. They'd want to keep me as long as they could, hope that it would make me start talking. Or maybe they just wanted to piss me off. I knew which one of them would eventually happen.

"Yes," Henley answered honestly. "I think they're going to schedule you for arraignment tomorrow morning."

I nodded. "Can you let Jasper know?"

My chest tightened at the thought of him. I didn't want to think about spending the night here, being without him. I already knew I didn't sleep well away from him. This was going to be so much worse.

"I'll call him first thing," Henley promised.

I nodded again. "Arraignment is when they decide if I get bail, right?"

"It is." Henley shifted in his chair. "I don't see a

130

judge remanding you, not with evidence this weak. But if the Lockwoods are putting some political pressure on, I doubt you'll be let out ROR."

"That means without having to pay bail, right?" I asked.

Henley nodded. "Now, because the trust is still being contested, you won't be able to use it to post bail, but you do have the vineyard and your own bank account, so I'll make sure everything is ready to get you out as soon as the judge gives us a number."

"Then what?"

"Then you go home and I do my job. I've already got a couple criminal attorneys lined up to help me with some things."

I thanked Henley and we went through a couple other things before he gave the detectives the go ahead to come back in. After that, things went exactly how he predicted. The cops asked questions and I gave the same answers I'd given a million times before. When they started to repeat their questions again, Henley intervened and told them that I was done.

I spent the rest of the day and the night in what Detective Rheingard called a holding cell. I didn't know what made it different from any other cell, but I really didn't care. Fortunately, the only other people in the cell were a drunk woman who snored, and a thirty-something woman who was wearing a dress that made me believe she'd been arrested for prostitution.

I didn't sleep well that night, but at least Henley

brought me clean clothes to change into for the arraignment, so I was able to make myself presentable before I was escorted into the courtroom. It helped me keep my head up and my shoulders squared as I was put behind the defendants' table.

"What are you asking for?" The judge sounded almost bored as she spoke to the prosecutor.

"Mrs. Lockwood is charged with the premeditated murder of her husband in order to seize his assets and continue her affair with her husband's best friend."

"Miss Donaldson is presenting information that has no evidence to support it," Henley interjected.

"Get to the point, Miss Donaldson," the judge said.

"The defendant has no local ties and the means to flee the country. We're asking for remand."

"My client has a job and a home here, and is more than willing to surrender her passport."

"A job that she's been suspended from," Miss Donaldson interrupted.

"That's enough." The judge held up a hand. "Two million, cash or bond and the defendant will surrender her passport." The gavel banged. "Next."

Jasper was waiting for me when I walked out, the bags under his eyes telling me he'd slept as well as I had. He wrapped me in his arms, and I sighed as I pressed my face against his chest. He kissed the top of my head.

"I've got you." His voice was low. "It's going to be okay."

I squeezed him tight. "Take me home."

He pulled me back far enough to kiss my forehead. "Of course." He wrapped his arm around my shoulders and turned us towards the doors. "Let's go."

.

134

Chapter 16

"You did what?" I stared at Jasper as he drove us home. I had to have heard him wrong.

"I used the clinic as collateral for your bail," he repeated. "I didn't want you to find out from Henley." He reached over and took my hand.

"Why didn't you use the vineyard or put up whatever the percentage was from my bank account?"

Jasper's mouth tightened. "The Lockwoods managed to do some legal shit I don't understand to make it so you couldn't put the vineyard up for collateral, and to freeze your savings account. You still have enough in checking to be fine for a while, and I'm sure Henley will be able to get the rest reversed in a couple days, but there wasn't enough for bail right away." He glanced at me, his expression dark. "And I wasn't about to let you stay in there a minute more than you had to."

"You didn't have to put up the clinic though," I protested.

"Are you planning on running?" he asked, one side of his mouth tilting up in a partial smile.

"No," I said, but couldn't help it. My lips curved

into a tiny smile.

"Then I don't have to worry about it, do I?" He raised our hands and pressed his lips against my knuckles. "Do you really think I would've let you sit in jail for days while Henley sorted this all out?"

"I don't know," I said, half-teasing. "Maybe you were getting tired of me."

"Never." His fingers tightened around mine. As he slowed to a stop at a red light, he looked over at me, his gaze intense. "I'll never be tired of you."

I squeezed his hand, trying to let him see on my face all of what I was feeling, everything I felt for him.

"We're going to get to the bottom of this," he said as he drove on. "I promise. You and me. We're in this together."

We didn't say anything for the rest of the ride and after how loud the drunk in the cell had been snoring all night, I was glad for the silence. The quiet lasted until we reached the door to the house.

"I cleaned up as best I could, but..." Jasper let his voice trail off as he opened the door and took me inside.

The living room was trashed. Couch cushions flipped, drawers opened, dvds scattered on the floor.

"The whole place was like this when I got home," Jasper said. I could hear the anger in his voice. "The cops tore up everything."

"It's okay," I said softly. It wasn't okay. It was far from fucking okay, but I couldn't let Jasper feel like this was his fault in any way.

"It's not."

I looked up at him, surprised at the intensity in his voice.

"It's not okay that they were able to do this." He turned until he was standing in front of me. He put his hand on my cheek and I leaned into his touch. "I hate that they can treat you like this and there's nothing I can do."

"You're doing enough," I said.

He sighed. "I started putting things together again based on the rooms I thought you'd need the most when you came home."

"Meaning?"

"Meaning our room is put back together, and so is our bathroom. I got most of the kitchen taken care of too." He gave me a rueful smile. "I didn't sleep much last night."

"Me either," I said.

"So let's get something to eat and spend the rest of the day in the bedroom. We have a lot to talk about."

I raised an eyebrow.

"That too." He grinned. "But first, food."

I didn't even want to see the rest of the house, but there was one thing I need to check. While Jasper went into the kitchen to get us something to eat, I went to the office. It was still a mess and I knew it would take days to even get close to being organized again. I wasn't sure what the cops had been looking for, but they'd gone through everything.

And my computer was gone. So was Allen's laptop.

I sighed. Neither one was really a surprise, but I'd been hoping that at least my computer would've been left. I'd have to go down and check the vineyard office at some point. I hadn't had enough time to read the search warrant to see if it had included anything there. I hoped not since that was where I'd moved my copies of Allen's letter and the email after my previous encounter with the police. I didn't think the cops here were corrupt, but I'd definitely wanted to have copies of my own for safe-keeping. Besides, the letter had sentimental value.

"Why don't you get cleaned up?" he called from the kitchen. "I'll bring the food to the bedroom."

I wave of gratitude swept over me. More than I wanted to eat, I wanted to be clean. I stepped under the hot spray and closed my eyes, letting it work into my stiff muscles as I began to scrub away the grime. By the time I stepped out of the shower, my skin was practically glowing, nearly raw. But at least I felt clean.

I pulled on my robe, sighing at the feel of the soft cotton against my skin. When I went into the bedroom, Jasper had a plate waiting for me. I climbed onto the bed and he handed it to me before taking the seat next to me. We ate without speaking, letting the sound from an old movie fill the silence. It was one I liked, an old black-and-white about a rabbit. I'd seen it more than a dozen times, which made it a good choice since I didn't exactly have to concentrate on it to be able to follow what was happening.

As the credits began to roll, Jasper spoke, "I

didn't just spend yesterday cleaning up."

I moved closer to him and he put his arm around me, pulling me close to his chest. I put my hand on his stomach, my fingers tracing lazy patterns as his muscles twitched beneath his t-shirt. "What else did you do?" I asked.

"I went down to the vineyard office to see if they'd searched there. Jacques was still there. He said he'd come in to check the wine just a few minutes after the cops arrived and figured he'd better stick around. It was a good thing he did because they did try to get into the office, but he read the search warrant and it was only for the main house."

I let out a breath I didn't know I'd been holding.

"He also found a copy of Allen's letter and a print-out of what looked like an email between Allen and me."

"I made copies and took them to the office, just in case," I admitted. "I just wish I would've copied that medical file too so you could see it."

"That would make things easier," Jasper agreed. "But I did read the email and I don't know who wrote it, but it wasn't me."

"I believe you." I looked up at him so he could see my face. "And I should have believed you before."

He kissed my forehead. "Forgiven and forgotten."

"Do you know who could've written it?" I asked, returning my attention to the firm muscles under my hand. I was tempted to pull up his shirt so I could feel his skin, but I didn't want to distract him.

Yet.

"I'm not sure," he said. "I mean, it was sent from my email account, so I suppose someone could've hacked it. I just don't know who."

"Do you think the Lockwoods could've hired someone to do it?"

"I thought about it," he said. He wasn't exactly frowning, but he had that little crease between his eyes that he got when he was thinking hard about something. "But there's something about it that I can't put my finger on, like I should recognize it even though I didn't write it."

I reached up and took his hand in mine. "We could tell the cops that you didn't write the email and they should be able to do some techie thing and figure out where it actually came from, right?"

"I suppose," he said. "But they might want my laptop for that."

I looked up and was surprised to see a flush creeping up his neck. I pushed myself up so that I was sitting. "Would that be a problem?"

His thumb was making circles on the back of my hand, and he was watching it intently. "Since I didn't send it, there wouldn't be anything on the hard drive, and they could check my email account from anywhere. They wouldn't need the laptop."

"But you don't want them to have it?" I pulled my hand away from his and gripped his chin, bringing his face up so I could see his eyes. "What, do you have porn on your computer?" I teased, wanting him to see that I wasn't accusing him of anything.

His flush deepened.

"Seriously?" I laughed. "I'm sure they'll find some on Allen's too."

"No." He shook his head. "That's not it."

Now I was intrigued. "What then? Why wouldn't you want the cops digging in your laptop?"

"I write things." His eyes slid away from mine. "It's not a journal or anything – or maybe it is – I don't know. When I can't think, I write stuff down to clear my head."

"Okay?" I'd never seen Jasper this uncomfortable before. "I still don't understand."

His gaze came back to mine, carefully guarded. "You've always been the reason I can't think clearly."

My hand dropped from his chin. "Oh."

He tucked my hair behind my ear. "From the moment I met you, you've been in my head. And since I could never do anything about it, I wrote. Wrote about you. How I felt."

My stomach tightened. He'd recently admitted how he'd been in love with me even when Allen and I had been together, but hearing it this way...it was different.

"There are files in there all the way back to the beginning," he said. "Places where I write how jealous I was of Allen and how hard it was pretending that all I felt for you was friendship. How torn I was because I loved Allen, and knew what a great guy he was, how much he loved you, but that I wanted you for myself."

He twisted a strand of hair around his finger, his

141

expression taking on a faraway look. I stared at him, unable to imagine how I could've missed it. Had he been that good at hiding or had I really been that blind?

"So, I think the cops will see what I wrote as evidence that either I killed Allen because of how I felt about you, or that the two of us were having some sort of affair. More than that, I don't want them reading the things I wrote about you." His finger stroked down my cheek.

"I understand," I said softly. He was right. If the cops read anything about how he wanted me before Allen died, they'd think the same things I thought when I first found out how he'd felt.

"No," he said. "You don't." His fingertip traced my bottom lip. "I don't just mean how I felt – how I feel – about you. If it was only that, it'd be different because it would only be me being exposed. The fantasies I used to have about you would have been bad enough..."

Something clicked. "You have new entries."

He nodded, looking away again, his cheeks suffused with color. "I write down everything. Every moment with you because I never want to forget it."

I thought about the first time we'd had sex. When he'd gone down on me in the living room. Making love outside. Me taking him in my mouth. The different positions...blood rushed to my face as I remembered how his cock had felt in my ass.

"Hey." Jasper cupped the side of my face. "Don't worry about it. I'll get rid of it. All of it."

I shook my head. "We'll figure out a way to keep

those files away from the cops, but I don't want you to throw them away."

His eyebrows went up as I got onto my knees. I leaned forward and brushed my lips against his.

"I believe you said something about fantasies you'd had?" I gave him a wicked smile. "I think I'd like to hear a bit more about those."

His eyes darkened as his mouth curved into a grin. "Well, there's this one I had involving whipped cream..."

"I think we have some left over from last week."

Chapter 17

Jasper offered to stay home with me until this was all worked out, but I told him to go back to the clinic. He'd already taken off the day I'd been released and I knew I'd want him there if the DA decided to take this to trial. Home by myself would be a lot easier than going to trial by myself.

I didn't want to think about that though. I knew if I stayed in bed late, that's what would happen. I wouldn't be able to stop thinking, and then I'd start to wallow and I'd be miserable.

When the alarm went off for Jasper to get up, I let myself doze a bit, but as soon as he came out of the bathroom, I forced myself up and into the shower. He was gone by the time I got out, but he'd left a heart drawn in the steam on the mirror. I was still smiling about it while I made myself breakfast.

It was funny, I thought, how I'd known Jasper for nearly a decade and never realized what a romantic he was. Because he'd never brought a lot of girlfriends around, and rarely the same girl twice, I always assumed he preferred to play the field. Yesterday, however, I learned that the real reason was that he'd never been able to find a girl who'd

145

made him forget me, and he'd felt it wasn't fair to them to be in a relationship with someone whose heart was somewhere else.

Heat swept through me as I remembered the other things we'd talked about yesterday. Talked about and done. The whipped cream had only been the beginning and I had the aches and bruises to prove it. He was much more imaginative than I ever realized.

Once we'd showered and made our way back into the bedroom, I told him that he hadn't needed to share anything with me he wasn't comfortable having me know, but he'd pulled out his laptop and had let me read everything. More than once I'd been moved to tears by the things he'd said, the way he'd seen me. Then there had been the entries where he'd talked about how he was grateful I'd found someone like Allen, how I deserved someone so much better than he was. My heart had broken at the way he saw himself, and I promised I'd do everything in my power to make sure he understood how special and amazing he was.

One way I'd decided to do that was to give Jasper every fantasy he'd had over the years, sexual and non-sexual. It would take a while to get to them all – eight years was a lot of time to fantasize – but we'd gotten a start last night. The whipped cream had been first, but it hadn't been the last. He'd taken me in a couple new positions, and had made me scream so loud that my throat was scratchy this morning.

A couple of his fantasies would have to wait until

summer since they involved things like making out on the beach and skinny dipping at midnight, but there were a few that had involved Christmas and New Year's, and that was where I was determined to go next.

First, that meant seeing how much decorating I could handle. Step one to that was going into the attic and taking a look at the boxes up there. It was a full attic, complete with heat and air so it could be used as an extra bedroom. Allen and I hadn't really needed the extra space for anything specific, so we'd used it for storage instead of the smaller crawlspace attic above the garage.

A dusty love-seat still sat against the wall, its fabric worn and faded. It had been the first piece of furniture we'd bought together for Allen's apartment near UCLA, and when he'd moved in here, he'd brought it with him even though his uncle had left all of his furniture to Allen along with the house. We'd come up here more than once to make love on it.

I picked up one of the boxes of decorations and carried it over to the love-seat and sat down. I opened it, bracing myself for the tide of emotion, but when it came, it wasn't as strong as I'd feared.

I pulled out garland, smiling as I remembered the first time Allen and I had tried to wrap it around the hand-rail leading up to the second floor. I still wasn't entirely sure how we'd managed to get it so wrong, but we'd ended up sitting on the stairs, tangled up in garland, laughing so hard that tears had been running down our cheeks. And then we'd had sex right there on the stairs.

I set the garland aside. I could use it.

I reached back into the box and found the wreath we'd hung on the front door of the vineyard office. It was hideous, a gift from May Lockwood after she'd made some comment about our taste in décor. Allen hadn't wanted to offend his mother, but neither one of us had wanted it on the house, so we'd put it at the office and Allen had told his mother that he'd thought it was perfect to greet his clients.

Neither one of us had ever mentioned that we didn't see clients in December, or that we barely went to the office ourselves in the winter either, so no one was really going to see it.

I put that to the other side. There was no way in hell I was keeping that thing now. I was half-tempted to burn it outside for the irony.

The house lights were at the bottom of the box and I put the garland back on top of them. I'd have to ask Jacques for help with those. I wasn't going to attempt to put them up on my own. I'd tried it one year, wanting to surprise Allen, and had fallen off the ladder and broken my arm. I knew Jasper would remember the incident, and be furious if I attempted to hang the lights myself again.

I pushed that box over to the stairs for me to take down when I was done. At least we'd have lights up and garland on the stair railing. It was a start.

I picked up another box and began to go through it. I was pleasantly surprised at how many decorations prompted fond memories, but nothing that made my heart ache badly enough that I couldn't bear to see them. I knew I wouldn't be able to handle the Christmas ornaments or the tree Allen and I had bought together, but at least the rest of the house would be decorated.

I was down to the last item in the last box when I found it.

Tucked inside the mouth of the nutcracker Allen and I had found at a garage sale two years ago was a small piece of paper.

Clue #1: Inside out. Upside down.

I stared at it, unable to believe what I was seeing. I blinked. Closed my eyes, and then opened them again. It was still there. Six words in Allen's handwriting. A clue. We'd always liked playing games. Board games, trivia games...we even liked watching detective shows together to see if we could figure out who the killer was before the detective did. Then, last year, during a conversation I couldn't really remember, Allen had jokingly threatened to hide my Christmas presents and make me solve clues to find them.

And now I couldn't believe that he'd done it. But it didn't make any sense. Allen and I would've found it together the day after Thanksgiving if he'd still been alive. If it had been my Christmas presents he'd wanted to hide, he would've wanted to wait until closer to Christmas to hide the clues so I couldn't find anything early.

Unless this wasn't about that. It hit me hard enough to make me gasp. Had Allen hidden these clues before he'd killed himself, knowing that I'd find them at Christmas and they'd lead me to something he wanted me to have?

One thing was for sure. I wasn't about to let it go. No matter what showed up at the end, even if it was nothing, I owed it to Allen and myself to go through with it.

The first clue was simple enough. I hadn't brought much with me when I'd moved in, but I had brought a couple boxes of childhood keepsakes, including my favorite books. One of which used the two phrases from the note.

I stood and walked to the far back corner where my boxes stood. If only I could remember which one the book was in. I looked at them, trying to decide if Allen would've put the box back on the top of the pile or if he would've assumed I'd go for the top box and put it lower in the pile, just to make things more difficult.

I opened the top box, took a quick peek and then set it aside. That was all of Mitchell's stuff. I had more storage room than he did, so I'd taken his things as well when he'd sold our parents' house.

The second box was the winner. The book was right on top. I opened it and the note was written right on the inside.

Clue #2: Paris 1821.

I frowned. History wasn't one of Allen's hobbies, and we'd never gone to Paris, or even talked about going, so there wasn't any sort of personal connection to the city. What would Paris 1821 mean?

I felt like an idiot when I realized what it was.

Wine.

Of course, it had something to do with wine.

I folded up the first note and put it in my pocket, then headed back downstairs. I went into the wine cellar first, looking at the label of each one until I found it. Under the bottle was another note.

Final Clue: The monkey chased the weasel. 32-15-27-08

A part of me wondered if Allen had been high on some sort of medication when he wrote this last one. Then the answer hit me and laughter bubbled up and out. I shook my head, still laughing as I headed for the stairs.

I pulled on my coat and slipped on a pair of tennis shoes. It wasn't freezing out, but the wind was still cool enough that I was glad for the extra layer, even for the distance between the house and the office. Jacques's car was parked it its usual spot, but he wasn't in the office. That wasn't surprising. He was most likely checking the wine vats like he did every day.

I didn't go looking for him. I'd talk to him about the lights tomorrow. What I wanted was in here and it was more important than the lights at the moment.

Hanging behind Allen's desk was a large picture of a tree. Or, at least, it was supposed to be a tree. It had been a running joke between the two of us. We'd seen the picture at a flea market and had started arguing about whether it was a tree or a bush. For some reason, it had struck us as funny and we'd bought the picture. Allen had insisted it was a maple tree. I'd said it was a mulberry bush. Like the one from the nursery rhyme...about a monkey chasing a weasel.

I took the picture off the wall and there it was, a small safe. I turned the dial left, then right, then each again, stopping at the numbers Allen had written down. When I got to the last one, I took a deep breath, my heart hammering in my chest. With trembling fingers, I pulled it open.

Chapter 18

It wasn't very big, but it didn't need to be to hold what was inside. A small, wrapped box sat on top of an envelope. I took both out and looked at them. I didn't need to see my name written on both, but there it was. One on a small tag on the box, the other on the envelope.

Neither one was typed. The handwriting matched the notes I'd found, but I would've know it anyway. It was Allen's. He'd always made fun of Jasper for his "doctor's scrawl," but his own had only been decent when he'd concentrated on making it that way.

Part of me wanted to rip into the letter here and now, but I knew that probably wasn't the best idea. I didn't know what the letter said, but I knew I'd want to read it in private. While the office was empty now, I didn't know when Jacques would be coming back, and I didn't want to be in the middle of something emotional when he did.

I put the box and the letter in the pocket of my coat, then headed back up to the house at a regular pace. I forced myself to take off my shoes and put them away, then hung up my coat before I took the gift and the envelope, and went to the couch. I considered taking them upstairs, but a part of me felt weird at the idea of reading something from Allen in the bed where I'd been sleeping with Jasper.

I sat down on the couch and put the little wrapped box on the coffee table. I wanted to open it, but I wanted to read the letter first.

My hands were shaking, making my name jump as I stared at the envelope. I wanted to read it, but I also didn't. The last time I'd read something that was supposed to have been from Allen, it had blown up in my face.

Then again, I had no way of definitely knowing where those other things had come from. I wanted to believe that letter I'd gotten in the mail had been from Allen, but it had been typed, even my name on the front.

The one I held in my hand had Allen's handwriting. It was from him. No doubt about it.

I opened the envelope and unfolded the letter, letting my eyes skim over the paper without actually reading anything at first. I just wanted to make sure that it was all handwritten. No point in getting my hopes up if it wasn't from him. But there it was, scrawled at the bottom. Two words I never thought I'd see in his handwriting again.

Love, Allen

I went back to the top, but I had to close my eyes for a moment, take slow breaths to try to steady my hands. It was going to be hard enough to read without it shaking all over the place.

When I opened my eyes again, the paper was

still.

Dear Shae,

I hope that by the time you find this, you'll have grieved enough that you won't hate me for what I'm about to tell you. Is that selfish of me? To wish that you won't hate me? I suppose it is, but it's hardly the only selfish thing I'll have done to you. And now I'm going to do it again because I can't handle the thought of you not knowing the truth.

I'm sick, love. I won't go into details, because I don't want you doing what I know you'd do and looking up everything you can find about the disease. Just know that it would've been horrible and I couldn't die like that. I couldn't make you watch me die like that.

Maybe suicide is the coward's way out. I'd always thought that, but it just goes to show that we never really know how we're going to handle something until it happens. I suppose I should've gone about it a different way, and I'm sorry that I couldn't think of anything else. Not without the insurance companies refusing to pay out. I know my parents are going to be a pain and I don't want to risk you being left with nothing.

Still, I know you must hate me for what I did. How I did it. Even more now that you know I did it on purpose. But please, Shae, don't hate me. I thought it was for the best.

The thing I regret the most is us talking about having kids when I knew that wasn't ever going to happen. I wanted nothing more than to have a family with you, Shae. To grow old with you.

Watch our children grow up. I know that will never happen, and it kills me to know it.

But you can have that future. Not with me, but you can still have it. Children. Grandchildren. Someone to spend your life with.

And here comes the next part where I think you're going to hate me.

Jasper.

Yes, he helped me fake my health records for the insurance company, but that's all he did. And he did it because he wants you to be taken care of. He loves you, Shae. He's loved you since we first met. He probably thinks I don't know, but I see it on his face every time he looks at you.

I know you've never thought of him as anything but a friend, but I think the two of you would be good together. He loves you, and I think you could love him too. Even if it's not as anything more than a friend, please take care of Jas. I know he's going to figure out what I did as soon as it happens, and he's going to blame himself. He won't ask for help, not from you. He'll feel like he needs to take care of you, both because he loves you, and because he'll feel guilty.

I love you, Shae. So much. I wish things could be different, but I have hope that you will have a long, happy life with someone who loves you as much as I do. I want that for you. I want you to be happy. To love again.

I can only hope that you can understand what I did and why. And that you can forgive me. That is the one thing that I'm scared of. That you'll hate *me. Please don't. Remember the good, love. And I'll be watching out for you.*

Love, Allen

I sniffled and wiped at my cheeks as I read the letter again.

And again.

Tears dripped off my chin as I took it all in. This was Allen. My Allen. He really had killed himself, but this letter didn't sound like the other one. I could hear his regret. And then what he'd said about Jasper, how he'd known how Jasper felt about me. And that he wanted me to take care of Jas. That he wanted us to be together.

I leaned forward and set the letter down. I couldn't read it anymore. I would want to read it again, I knew, but not now.

The box was still sitting there, a small, flat thing with my name on it. A part of me didn't want to open it, wanted to save it forever. Almost as if keeping it wrapped and unopened would keep a piece of Allen for me.

I reached for it, my fingers tracing my name as I imagined him writing it. Imagined him wrapping the gift. I carefully slid my finger under the flap and began to work the paper off. I was never this gentle when I opened my gifts normally, but I wanted to save it. My last keepsake from him.

I set the paper down next to the letter and took a deep breath. The box was plain and black, nothing written on it to tell me where it was from. I opened it and caught my breath.

Inside, nestled against black velvet, was a small

silver spoon.

It wasn't something new. I knew that because I'd seen it before. Allen had shown it to me. It and a dozen other ones just like it.

They were Lockwood family silver spoons. Ones that the Lockwoods had engraved with every child and grandchild's name and birthdate.

There was a small piece of paper folded underneath it and I pulled it out.

It wasn't addressed to me.

Dear Baby Girl or Boy,

You don't know me, but I knew your mother. She is the most special person in the world, and I know she loves you more than anything else in the world. She's been thinking about having you for years, and I know now that you're here, she's going to be the best mom in the world. I don't know if I knew your dad, but I'm sure, no matter who he is, that your mother has picked someone amazing to share her life with. Be good to them because I know they love you more than anything.

I buried my face in my hands and cried.

Chapter 19

I was still crying when Jasper came home. These weren't gut-wrenching sobs or even the sort of hard, angry cry I'd experienced over the past six months. There was some sadness in the tears, but more a sense of relief and gratitude. Relief that I now knew for sure what had happened and how Allen had felt. Gratitude that I'd been allowed to have as much time with Allen as I'd had. Gratitude for everything I'd had with him.

"Shae." Jasper was at my side immediately, not even bothering to take off his coat.

I put my face against his broad chest and breathed in the scent of cold that clung to the fabric. The feel of his arms calmed me, and after a few moments, I pulled back to wipe my face.

"What is it?" he asked. "Did something else happen with the police?"

I shook my head. "No." I gestured towards the table.

"What's that?" He shifted so that one arm was around my shoulders and he could reach for the letter with the other.

"Read it," I said quietly. It was strange that the

159

thought of Jasper reading something so personal didn't bother me. In fact, I preferred him reading it to me having to explain it.

He pulled me tight against him as he settled back against the couch to read. I rested my head on his shoulder, not wanting to look at his face while he read. After a few minutes, I felt him sigh and he set the letter aside.

"Are you okay?" He smoothed down my hair.

I nodded. "Surprisingly, yes. I feel like this kind of weight was lifted off of me. Like I finally got answers."

"This is Allen's handwriting," he said quietly.

I straightened a bit, turning so I could look at him. I could hear what he wasn't saying. "I don't think the other letter was really from Allen."

He opened his mouth, hesitated, and then spoke, "I didn't want to say it before, but I agree. It didn't really sound like Allen. That other letter. But this, it sounds like him."

"It does," I agreed. "And that was with the letter." I pointed at the box.

Jasper reached out and opened the box. He stared at the spoon, the look on his face telling me that he knew exactly what it was. He read the note next and I watched him wipe his own eyes. He set the note down and gently touched the spoon.

"I can't believe he did that." There was a soft smile on his face. "No, actually, I can. That's exactly the kind of man Allen was."

"Do you think he knew?" I asked.

"Knew what?" He turned back to me.

"That this would happen." I leaned back into him and pulled his arm around me. "You and me. Do you think Allen knew that the two of us would end up together?"

Jasper kissed the top of my head. "I don't know. But he hoped we would. That the two people who loved him more than anything else would fall in love with each other."

"I want to decorate," I said suddenly. "I want to decorate the house for Christmas. And I want the two of us to spend the holiday together. I'll invite Mitchell to come over on Christmas Day for a bit, but I want it to be about the two of us."

I didn't ask if he wanted to invite his family. I already knew how he felt, and if something changed, I was sure he'd let me know.

"That sounds perfect." He cupped my chin and tipped my head up. "Anything with you sounds perfect." He brushed his lips across mine. A gentle kiss, but one that still made my stomach flip. "When do you want to decorate?"

I smiled at him. "Tomorrow. I have something else I'd like to do tonight."

I pushed myself up to press my mouth more firmly against his. He made a sound in the back of his throat as I slid my hands under his coat, pushing it off him. I let my hands linger on his broad shoulders as he pushed his hands under the bottom of my shirt, palms skimming over the small of my back and up my spine. His skin was still chilled from being outside.

His fingers curled over the clasp of my bra and

161

his teeth scraped over my bottom lip, drawing a moan from me. He broke the kiss, but didn't pull back.

"Bedroom." His voice was rough, twisting things low inside me. "Now."

I linked my fingers behind his neck. "We can stay here."

He shook his head, his eyes a dark, stormy gray. "I want to take it slow."

Oh.

He stood, reaching down to take my hand. He pulled me to my feet and the two of us walked upstairs and into our room. Once inside, he peeled off his shirt, revealing the sculpted torso and narrow hips that made my mouth water. I'd loved the way Allen had been built, but Jasper's body was equally as delicious.

I was so distracted by him that he was lowering his boxer-briefs when I finally remembered that I was still fully clothed. As he straightened, he smirked at me, the sort of self-satisfied smile that said he knew exactly what I'd been doing and that he enjoyed knowing it.

I started to reach for the bottom of my shirt, but his hands covered mine, stopping me. I raised my hands above my head and let him pull the shirt over and off. He let it drop to the floor and then stood there, looking at me with a hungry expression on his face.

"I'll never get tired of this," he said as he lightly ran his fingers along my collarbone, then down along my bra. "Seeing you. Touching you." He cupped my breast over my bra. "Knowing you're mine."

If he'd told me that before I'd read his journal, read how he'd felt about me for all these years, I would've appreciated the remark, but I couldn't have understood the enormity of what he meant. Now, I got it. Knowing how long, how patiently he'd waited for me, never knowing if he'd even have a chance to tell me how he felt, or if he did, if I'd return the feelings...it was almost overwhelming. I'd never doubted the depth of Allen's love for me, and I knew I could believe as strongly in what Jasper felt for me.

"How did I get so lucky?" I asked as I reached out and put my hand over his heart. "Most people think they're fortunate if they find one person who can love them the way I've been loved. And I've had two."

He covered my hand with his and held it there for a moment before pulling my hand up to kiss the palm. He released my hand and reached around behind me to open my bra clasp. He pulled it off and covered my breasts with his hands. His fingers moved over the soft flesh, and his thumbs ran back and forth across my nipples until the darker flesh was hard and tight.

"I imagined doing this so many times," he said, his gaze still on my breasts. "Touching you like this, seeing your body respond to me."

Heat unfurled in my belly, spreading out and around, saturating my skin, my muscles, every part of me. When he lowered his head and flicked his tongue across my nipple, I moaned.

"On the bed," he said, lifting his head.

I sat down on the edge and then pushed myself back until I was in the middle. He crawled up next to me, his movements graceful, sensual. Allen hadn't been awkward, but there was just something about the way Jasper moved that would've made me think of sex, even if he hadn't been naked.

He stretched himself out over my body, his bare skin pressed against my jeans, then against my bare skin. He placed open-mouthed kisses up my stomach, and then across my breasts, teeth and lips pulling at my skin until it turned pink. He sucked skin into his mouth and I ran my fingers through his hair, holding him at my breast as he marked me. His fingers were at my waist, fingers teasing at the flesh just below the edge of my jeans.

I gasped as he closed his mouth over my nipple. He sucked on it hard enough to make me cry out, back arching. Each pull was like a bolt of electricity straight to my core. Then he switched to the other, the air suddenly cold against my wet skin. His fingers were at work between us, deftly undoing my button and zipper. He raised himself up on one arm without breaking suction. His teeth scraped back and forth over my nipple as he shoved his hand into my pants, fingers working their way over my panties until they were pressed against the damp cotton.

"So wet," he murmured as he rubbed my clit though the material.

My eyes closed and his mouth returned to where it had been, teeth sharp as they nipped, tongue soothing. His fingers continued to apply that wonderful friction and my body began to tighten, building towards climax.

And suddenly I was there, crying out his name as I ground down on his hand, desperate for more. He pressed his fingers harder against me, his mouth suddenly at my ear.

"That's it, baby. Come on my hand. I love knowing that I brought you here with just my fingers." He bit my earlobe and my body jerked. "Now I'm going to bring you with my mouth, lick every inch of you until you're writhing with pleasure."

Fuck.

Before I could even consider how to respond to what he'd said, he was sliding down my body, pulling my jeans and panties off in the same smooth motion. He tossed them over his shoulder as he grabbed my ankles and pulled my legs apart. I didn't have time to be embarrassed by the sudden exposure because he was right there, desire clearly written on his face.

"I used to wonder about what you tasted like," he said. He pressed his lips against the inside of my thigh. "Wonder what it would be like to feel you come against my mouth."

I shivered. Jasper had never talked like this before, not about how he'd felt before. Maybe it had been Allen's letter saying that he wanted me to take care of Jasper, or maybe it had been him letting me read his journal, but something had changed to make him feel comfortable saying these things. Whatever the reason, I liked it. Not just because the things he was saying made me feel wanted, but because I wanted to know him, know how he felt and thought.

He ran the flat of his tongue across the sensitive skin and another shiver went through me. He wrapped his hands around my thighs, holding me in place as he pressed his mouth against me. I cried out, my body attempting to move, but his grip was tight, preventing me from going anywhere.

He was relentless, tongue sliding between my folds, dipping into me before moving up to tease my swollen clit. Each touch sent a new ripple of pleasure through me and then I was coming, my muscles tensing as the orgasm caught me by surprise. I grabbed the comforter in my fists, pulling at it as Jasper continued to lick even as I came. One climax rolled into another the moment his lips covered my clit and started to suck.

"Please, Jas," I began to beg as my body shook. "Please, please, please..." I wasn't even sure what I was begging for, only that I didn't think I could take much more.

I let out a half-sob of relief as he raised his head. He kissed my hip, then moved up until he was laying next to me. He wrapped his arms around me, pulling me against him, holding me until I stopped trembling.

"Do you have any idea what that does to me?" He pressed his lips against the top of my head. His voice was soft, his touch gentle as he ran his fingers over my shoulders. "Seeing you come apart like that. Hearing you say my name."

I ran my fingers across his chest, smiling as I scraped my nails over his nipple and he hissed. I moved my hand lower, across his flat stomach, and then wrapped my fingers around his cock. He made a sound halfway between a growl and a moan as I gripped him, rubbing my thumb across his soft skin.

"I love knowing that I make you hard," I said then kissed his chest. "I love hearing you say my name."

"Shae," he murmured, his hands tightening on my shoulders.

I looked up at him as I started to stroke his cock, my hand moving up and down his thick shaft in a slow and steady rhythm. Our eyes met, and he held my gaze for what felt like an eternity, like nothing existed outside of us, the feel of his body against mine, my hand moving over him.

Then, suddenly, he surged upright and pulled me across his lap. My legs automatically went on either side of him as he gripped my waist and held me up so that the tip of him was brushing against my entrance. He stretched his arm up along my spine, balancing me even as he slowly lowered me onto him.

My eyes closed as he entered me and he stopped.

"Open your eyes." His voice held an edge of something dark, almost dangerous.

I did and swallowed hard at the look on his face. It was full of raw emotions. Lust and desire that made every part of me heat up. Love so strong that it felt like I couldn't contain it all. And a possessiveness that twisted that primal part of me that wanted him to claim me.

We watched each other as my body slid down onto him, each inch bringing us that much closer to being joined as intimately as two people could be. My breath was coming in short pants by the time he was fully inside me, my body feeling like it had been stretched to the limit.

I wrapped my arms around his neck as his hands settled at the small of my back, waiting for me to adjust to the overly full feeling that always came with having him inside me. I began to rock against him and he responded, his body moving with mine. There were no deep, penetrating thrusts, but he was pressed against everything, every nerve singing with the pressure and friction of our dance. Neither of us spoke, letting our bodies say what we knew we had no words to express.

As my body began to tighten, he reached up and put his hand on my cheek, his thumb sliding into my mouth. I sucked on it, ran my teeth along the pad, circled it with my tongue. He made a small sound and then replaced his thumb with his finger. I repeated what I'd done, the salty taste of his skin bursting across my tongue.

When he dropped his hand behind me, his wet finger sliding between my cheeks, I sucked in a breath, knowing what was coming. I was already hovering on the edge, and I knew only a bit more sensation and I'd be tipping over. Then his finger was there, pressing against my asshole and I leaned forward, giving him the bit of space he needed to push his finger inside.

I swore as I came, deep shudders of pleasure running through me as he twisted his finger, the base of his cock rubbing against my clit almost painfully. I pressed my face to his shoulder, biting down on the hard muscle there.

His body jerked against mine and I heard him say my name. Then he was coming too, pulsing and spilling into me, the sensations sending another ripple of pleasure through me. I clung to him as we rode each others' bodies, wringing out every last drop of pleasure until we collapsed back onto the bed, spent.

Chapter 20

The day after I found Allen's real letter and gift, I brought down my Christmas decorations and spent the whole day putting them up. When Jasper came home, everything was up and I actually felt like it was the holidays.

I'd put the garland up the staircase railing, but everything else had gone somewhere new. It was the perfect combination of familiar and new, letting me use what Allen and I had bought, but not making the rooms look identical to how they'd been before.

The only thing I didn't do was put up the tree. It just felt like it'd be a bit strange to have all of those Christmas ornaments that Allen and I had collected during our time together. I had some of my own, but there weren't enough to cover the whole tree. And then there was the issue with the tree itself. It was shabby and probably should've been replaced a couple years ago, but it had sentimental value. But I didn't want that sentiment becoming a part of the new life I was sharing with Jasper. I wanted us to have our own traditions and our own things to be sentimental about. I just wasn't sure what I wanted to do about the tree. But it was only the first week in

December, so we had plenty of time to decide.

As much as I enjoyed spending all of Thursday decorating, I did find one downside to it on Friday morning.

I was bored out of my mind.

I didn't have any cleaning to do since I'd done that when I'd cleaned up after the cops had torn things up. My decorating was done. I made a batch of gingerbread men, but I was done before lunch and knew that if I started doing any serious baking, we'd be buried in food by the time Christmas came around. I had no schoolwork to do and there wasn't anything I needed to attend to at the vineyard.

I had no idea what I could do to keep myself busy, but I did know that if I didn't find something else to do, I was going to lose my mind. I'd done most of my shopping online already, but there were always a few things I could pick up. With that decided, I headed out.

I was halfway into the city when I remembered I hadn't taken the time to eat lunch. On a whim, I decided to run through and pick something up to take to Jasper so we could have lunch together.

Georgia was at the desk when I came in, and I forced myself to give her a smile. Her hand was still wrapped and I felt a pang of annoyance. It was probably petty of me, I knew, to think she'd done it on purpose, but I couldn't help it. Something in my gut just made me not want to like her.

"I brought lunch for Jasper." I held up the bag.

"Dr. Whitehall has patients for the next half hour." She gave me that smile I hated.

"Then I'll go wait in his office with it." I opened the door to the lobby and headed down the hall before she could make some sort of protest or excuse as to why I shouldn't be there.

I stuck the bags in the refrigerator and sat down behind Jasper's desk. I pulled out my phone and started flipping through a Christmas cookbook I'd downloaded. Allen and I used to have ham for Christmas, but I'd never been overly fond of it. He'd been the one who liked it. Sort of like the whole wine versus beer thing. Now I was looking for something that would go well with beer. Maybe turkey or I could get ambitious and do a duck or goose. I wasn't even sure if I liked duck or goose, but I figured I could try before Christmas, and find out what Jasper and I liked.

"Hey, babe," Jasper said as he walked in. He smiled at me. "I didn't know you were here."

It didn't surprise me that Georgia hadn't told him. I stood and went to him, kissing his cheek. "I was going to go out and maybe pick up a couple things, and I realized I hadn't eaten lunch yet. I figured I'd bring you something and we could eat together."

"Perfect." He smiled and put his arms around my waist. "I was just going to order something anyway."

He bent his head and kissed me soundly, heat spreading through me. It wasn't a long kiss, but it was a thorough one and my pulse was racing by the time he let me go.

Damn. I loved that he could do that.

173

"I got sandwiches," I said as I walked back to the fridge. "Figured they could be either hot or cold since I didn't know when you were going to be free."

When I turned back around, Jasper was sitting in his chair. I walked over to hand him a bag, and he took it with one hand, wrapping the other arm around my waist and pulling me down on his lap. I laughed, letting myself relax into him as we put our bags on the desk.

"Did you want the grilled chicken or the roast beef?" I asked.

"Surprise me."

He wrapped his other arm around me and rested his chin against my shoulder. I opened one of the bags and pulled out a sandwich. He took it and I took the other one. We ate in comfortable silence.

"Did you have somewhere specific you wanted to go today?" Jasper asked as he finished his sandwich.

"Not really," I said. "Why?"

"I was thinking you could stay and take a look through some old paperwork I haven't been able to go through yet." He reached up and tucked some hair behind my ear. "I'm trying to find Allen's real test results."

"I thought you had everything sorted already," I said.

"Yes and no." He brushed the back of his hand down my arm. "Everything's put away." He gestured towards some filing cabinets standing against the far wall. "But I had Georgia doing a lot of that filing, and I didn't want to ask her to look through them for this."

"What about doctor-patient confidentiality?" I asked.

"Oh, those aren't medical records. They're billing for medical equipment, stuff like that," he explained. "I've looked through the medical records to see if Allen's tests had been misfiled there, but they weren't. Now I'm wondering if they accidentally got put in with all of that extra stuff."

"And it'd be okay for me to go through them?"

He nodded. "Unless you had something you needed to do today."

I shook my head. "Not particularly. I'd just figured I'd go out because it was going to drive me nuts sitting at home for the rest of the afternoon." I smiled sadly. "I'm not used to not being busy."

"You'll be back in school before you know it." He wrapped his fingers around mine and squeezed. "You'll be grading papers and praying for summer."

"I hope so." I ran my fingers through his hair. "I miss the kids."

"I know you do." He brushed his lips across mine.

I sighed and rested my forehead against his for a moment. I knew he had to get back to work soon, but I was glad for the few moments here when I could feel like even the crazy problems we had were going to be okay.

After a minute or so, I climbed off his lap and headed over to the filing cabinets. He came over and kissed my cheek. "I'll stop in when I can."

It wasn't the most thrilling work in the world. It wasn't even as exciting as grading spelling tests. In fact, it was mind-numbing, but at least it was keeping me busy. I didn't want to rush and possibly miss something, so I took my time, looking at each one until I was certain that I wasn't reading anything to do with Allen.

Every so often, Jasper would stop in, give me a quick kiss and ask if I was staying a bit longer. It was nice, knowing he was there.

I was halfway through the next to last drawer when I found it. Found them. The first one was an x-ray with Allen's name on it. The others were behind it, various tests and notes that I knew I wouldn't completely understand. I took the papers out and went over to Jasper's desk. I sat down and stacked them neatly in front of me. I looked up at the clock. It was nearly five-thirty. Jasper would be finishing up soon.

I looked down at the papers and began to flip through them. Most of the medical jargon I didn't understand, but there was enough I could. It didn't take long for me to know for certain that these were Allen's real records. And he really had been sick.

When I reached the last page, there was a sticky note on the top that told me everything I needed to know.

Creutzfeldt-Jakob. No cure. Fast.

That first letter I'd received had named the disease. That was it. Allen had been dying and there was no cure.

Whoever had written that first letter had known two things. Somehow they knew that Allen killed himself, but, just as confusing, they knew the name of the disease that had already been taking him from me.

Chapter 21

"Shae?" Jasper sounded concerned as he entered his office and saw me sitting there.

"I found them." I gestured to the papers. "Allen's real test results."

He leaned against the desk. "Are you okay?"

I pushed aside the top ones and tapped the sticky note. "Allen had Creutzfeldt-Jakob disease."

"I know," Jasper said, a puzzled expression on his face as he glanced down at the tests. "I've seen these reports before."

"So did the person who wrote the first letter."

His eyes widened and he looked back down at the papers, finally seeing where I was pointing.

"Whoever wrote that first letter knew the exact name of the disease that Allen had. Neither of us thought anything of it when we first heard it because we assumed Allen had written it. Of course he'd know what he had."

"But Allen didn't write that letter," Jasper said slowly.

"I know." My mind was spinning. "We know that now."

"But whoever did..." Jasper's voice trailed off.

"Fuck."

"We need to find out who else had access to these tests," I said. "Or who they could've told—"

"I know who did it." His voice was quiet, but it stopped my sentence cold.

I looked up at him. His skin was pale, a stricken expression on his face. "Who?"

"Georgia."

I stared at him. Was he serious?

"That's her handwriting." He tapped the note my finger was resting on. "Look at what it says, Shae. 'Creutzfeldt-Jakob. No cure. Fast.'"

The words echoed in my head. They'd sounded familiar before, but I still couldn't figure out why.

"That's what the letter said," Jasper said quietly. "Those exact words. I'd thought before that the style of the letter sounded familiar, and now I know why. It was Georgia. She wrote that letter, but I don't know why."

I shook my head. "She's in love with you." His head jerked up and I chuckled at the expression on his face. "Or she's at least infatuated with you."

"Shit," he muttered. Color flooded his face. "I went out with her...or, well, we hooked up."

"What?" I had to have heard him wrong. There was no way he'd just said that he'd slept with Georgia Overstreet.

"When I first started working with my dad, I asked her out." He rubbed the back of his neck. "She was cute and liked me. That was pretty much all I needed at the time." He gave me a rueful look. "It was hell trying to get you out of my head."

180

Dammit. "Did she know that's why you went out with her?"

He paused for a moment and then shrugged. "I didn't think so, but now I think she might have."

I let out a breath. "So what do we do now?"

He looked down at me. "I have an idea."

***

"This is where Georgia lives?" I looked at the house and rubbed my hands together. I'd worn my coat, but I hadn't realized it'd be cold enough for gloves this early in the morning.

"It's the address on her application," Jasper said.

By the time the two of us had decided exactly how we would handle the situation, Georgia had already left for the night. Since there were some other things that we had to work out, we decided to wait until the next morning to confront her.

Now it was early Saturday morning and the two of us were standing in front of a little cottage-type house painted the ugliest shade of green I'd ever seen. The front lawn was neatly trimmed and dotted with garden gnomes. There must've been at least fifty, and each one had that creepy smile that those sorts of decorations always seemed to have.

"Are you sure you're okay doing this?" Jasper asked as he reached over and took my hand.

"I just want to get to the bottom of all of this so we can get on with our lives." I returned the comforting squeeze of his fingers.

"All right." He released my hand and started up the narrow walkway that led to the front steps.

I fell in step behind him and resisted the urge to reach out and touch him. We'd both agreed that if Georgia really had done this, and she had a thing for Jasper, it would be better if she didn't see us being physically affectionate with each other. It would be bad enough that we were there together. Jasper had wanted to go in alone, but I'd been adamant that I go with him. I hadn't told him my suspicion that Georgia had cut her hand on purpose to get his attention, but it was starting to feel a lot less like petty jealousy on my part, and more like pieces were falling into place.

He rang the doorbell, and less than a minute later, the door opened. Georgia was wearing a pair of flannel pajama pants and a flimsy camisole top that looked like it had seen better days. Her short hair stood up in weird clumps all over her head. As soon as she saw Jasper, her face flushed red and I almost felt bad for her. If we were wrong about her, then I would feel bad. At the moment, though, I was thinking more about everything she'd put us through and sympathy wasn't exactly high on my priority list.

"Jasper! I mean, Dr. Whitehall..." Her hand went to her hair. "What a pleasant surprise. I wasn't expecting company so early in the morning." Her eyes darted over to me and her mouth flattened. "Mrs. Lockwood."

"Miss Overstreet." I nodded at her, but didn't smile.

"I have a couple things I'd like to talk to you about." Jasper drew her attention back to him with a charming smile. "May we come in?"

Her eyes darted to me and I knew she was torn. She wanted Jasper to come inside, but she didn't want me, and there wasn't any way to give him permission and exclude me without looking bad.

"Of course." She stepped aside and motioned for us to come in. "Please excuse the mess. I didn't have a chance to tidy up."

As I followed Jasper inside, I had to admit that I had no idea what mess she was talking about. The place was spotless. Judging by the smell of bleach lingering in the air, she'd made sure it was germ-free as well. That, at least, was a pleasant surprise. I'd been expecting her to live in piles of filth, with thirty cats and the permeating smell of urine and feces. The lack of these things wasn't proof that she wasn't crazy or obsessed, but I did feel bad that I'd come up with such a stereotypical image.

"Would you like something to drink?" she asked as we sat down on the couch. She didn't specifically address Jasper, but her body language made it quite clear that he was the one she was talking to.

"No, thank you," he said politely. He gestured towards the chair next to where he was sitting.

She sat down, crossing her legs as she leaned towards Jasper. "You said you needed to talk to me about something?"

I tried not to hold my breath. This was where things would get tricky. If Jasper came out and accused her, there was a good chance she'd clam up and not say anything. We'd carefully worked out the wording, but all of it depended on how desperate she was to believe whatever Jasper told her.

"I'm in a bit of trouble," he began. "The police think that Shae and I killed Allen because we were having and affair and wanted his money."

"But that's not true!" Georgia exclaimed. "You'd never do anything like that."

"Thank you. I'm glad you see that," he continued. "But earlier this week, they arrested Shae and searched the house."

The look she gave me clearly said that she had no problem with this particular part of the story.

"They found some things that implicate me in Allen's death. A letter that Shae had gotten from Allen after he died. It says that I'd helped him lie to the insurance company so he could get a big insurance policy. Then they got onto Allen's laptop, and there was an email from me to him that made it sound like I encouraged him to get the policy. The same policy that helped me get the clinic up and running. And then they found medical records that show Allen was perfectly healthy." Jasper made a frustrated sound. "I told them that none of those were real, but no one believes me." He gestured towards me. "Not even her."

"I believe you," she said. She reached out and put her hand on Jasper's knee. "You were always such a good friend to Mr. Lockwood. I'm sure the police will realize that you never would have hurt him."

"That's the thing." Jasper didn't push her hand away. "The letter named the disease that Allen had, and the healthy medical records either prove that I lied to the insurance company or that I lied to Allen.

Either way, I'm screwed. The email just makes it that much worse."

"What do you need me to do?" Georgia asked. "I can tell the cops that Mr. Lockwood had Creutzfeldt-Jakob and that I heard you tell him that."

"But that just proves I lied to the insurance company."

"Not if you have Mr. Lockwood's real results," she countered. "I know where they are. I'll tell the police that the ones they have are old, or that I accidentally misfiled the new ones."

"Thank you, Georgia." Jasper smiled at her. "But the letter and the email both say that I knew Allen was sick and that I'd encouraged him to get the million dollar insurance policy. The real records will only support the cops' claims that I wanted Allen's money."

"Just tell them you didn't write the email or the letter."

I could see her body tensing with anxiety. This was what we'd wanted. To get her to admit what she'd done and why she'd done it.

"I told them that, but they have all this evidence that I did it. The fact that the letter names the disease when only a couple of people knew about it. The email was from my email address." He turned so that his back was to me. "They're going to arrest me, and I'm going to go to jail for something I didn't do."

"No you won't." She was clearly focused all on him. "I'll tell them that I did it."

"No." He shook his head. "I can't let you lie for

185

me. It wouldn't be right."

"But it's not a lie," she said earnestly, her fingers clutching his knee now. "I wrote and sent that letter. I paid Allyson Neely fifty dollars to post-date it and say that it had gotten lost in the mail."

"Why would you do that?" Jasper asked. "It got me in a lot of trouble."

She sighed and dropped her face in her hands. "I'm so sorry," she said. "That wasn't what I meant to happen. I'd heard you and Mr. Lockwood talking about him being sick and what you did to help him. When he died, I didn't want you to get in trouble, so I hid his real records."

"But you wrote a letter to Shae telling her what I did."

Georgia's cheeks flushed red. "I wanted her to get mad at you." Her voice dropped to a whisper. "She doesn't deserve you."

My nails bit into my palms, but I forced myself to stay still and quiet. She'd all but forgotten I was there. We needed her to keep talking.

"And I knew if I put in the letter what you'd done, she'd be upset, but she wouldn't go to the cops because she'd lose the insurance money if it came out that Mr. Lockwood had committed suicide."

"The cops aren't going to believe that you wrote that letter," Jasper said, pressing for more information. "They'll say you're just trying to protect me because I'm your boss."

"I can show them the original. It's still on my computer," she said. "I can't get arrested for writing a letter."

"They still have my email."

She shook her head. "I wrote it."

"How?" Jasper's voice was gentle rather than accusatory.

"You use the same password for your work email as you do for your personal one." She looked pleased with herself. "I just accessed your personal account, sent the email and then deleted it from your sent messages."

"But it was sent before Allen died."

She smiled. "No, it wasn't. When you didn't leave *her*, I knew I had to make you see that she didn't trust you. I called my nephew in Montana. He knows a lot about computers, and he told me how to make the date on the email different."

We had her. Everything that the police had to 'prove' that Jasper and I had conspired to kill Allen, she'd confessed to. The only thing the cops could arrest Jasper for was what had happened with the insurance company, but we'd worry about that later. Jasper had said he was willing to take his punishment for what he'd actually done. It was more important that neither of us were being charged with murder.

"Now I see how it all went wrong," Georgia said. "But I can fix it." She stood suddenly and smiled brightly at both me and Jasper. "I'm going to go get us some tea."

She left before either of us could refuse.

"Let's go," I said quietly. "We have everything we need."

"We don't want to make her suspicious," Jasper

said, his voice low. "We'll drink the tea and then tell her we need to go."

I nodded in agreement, trying to still the butterflies in my stomach. For some reason, my gut had decided that now was the time to be nervous. I didn't get it. We'd gotten a confession, and now all we had to do was drink some tea and get out of here.

A few minutes passed and Georgia came back in with a tea tray. She set it on the table and handed me the cup that already had tea in it.

"Here."

My stomach twisted and churned, threatening rebellion if I tried to put anything in it.

"That's okay," I said politely. "My stomach's a bit upset. Thank you anyway. We really do need to get going."

Georgia's smile tightened and she reached behind her, pulling out a small, but very real, gun. "Drink the tea, Mrs. Lockwood. Or things are going to get very unpleasant."

Chapter 22

When Jasper and I had decided to confront Georgia about forging the letter and email, I thought it might be possible for her to get upset and perhaps start screaming and yelling. Maybe she'd throw something or try to slap one of us. Scratch us with the claw-like fake fingernails she was sporting.

Nowhere in any of that had I thought she'd use a gun to force me into drinking a cup of tea. And I seriously doubted she was the kind of crazy who wanted me to drink the tea because we were all going to be such good friends.

"What's in it?" I asked, silently congratulating myself for not freaking out. On the outside at least.

Georgia's smile was decidedly unpleasant. "Try it and find out."

"Georgia." Jasper made his voice as soothing as possible, but I could feel the tension radiating off of him. "You don't need to do this."

"Oh, I think I do," she said. "It doesn't matter what I do, she's always there. Between us. So she has to go away. It's the only way we can be together."

"If you hurt her, Georgia, I'll never be with you," he warned.

"Yes, you will." She looked back at me. "Now drink. Or I'll shoot him." She slid her gun over to point at Jasper.

I didn't think she'd do it, but I wasn't willing to take that chance. Not with him.

"Don't do it, Shae." Jasper didn't take his eyes off of the gun. "She won't shoot me."

"I will," she countered. "I'll shoot you in the leg, and then I'll shoot her. And don't even think about throwing it out. I'll shoot you for that too."

"It'll be okay," I said quietly. "I love you, Jas."

I raised the cup, but before it reached my mouth, Jasper grabbed it. I started to reach for it, but he was already tipping it back, draining every last drop.

Georgia screamed, but I barely registered it. I only cared about one thing. I grabbed Jasper's shoulders.

"What were you thinking?!"

"I love you too. Always."

He gave me a smile that turned into a grimace. Georgia was still screaming as his eyes rolled back and he slumped against the couch. For one terrifying moment, I was too panicked to do anything. Then I heard Georgia yell his name, and it snapped me back to reality.

I dug into my pocket and dialed 911. I gave the operator the address as I stood and grabbed Georgia's arm. I shook her hard, but she didn't stop screaming. My hand came across her face with a crack hard enough to hurt my palm.

"What did you give him?" I asked. "Georgia!

What was in that cup?"

She stared at me with wide, wild eyes, and I knew, at that moment, that Jasper was going to die.

***

The cops had needed to sedate Georgia before they could drag her away from Jasper, and it was a good thing they had because I'd seriously been considering grabbing her gun and shooting her with it, if only to make her shut up. She was screaming and babbling about how she'd never meant to hurt him, and how much she loved him. The only thing that had kept me from getting myself arrested for homicide had been the pulse I'd still been able to feel under my fingers.

Detectives Reed and Rheingard had heard the call go out and had arrived just as Jasper was being loaded into the ambulance. When they'd told me that I had to answer questions before I'd be allowed to go with him, I'd flipped them both off as I'd followed Jasper into the ambulance. Probably not the most mature move on my part, but I'd had enough.

They'd been pissed when they'd arrived at the hospital, but I hadn't cared. I'd ignored their questions as I'd paced in front of the doors to the room where they'd taken Jasper. Then the doctor came out with news.

Georgia was fucking crazy, but she was completely inept when it came to poison.

They'd pumped Jasper's stomach, and wanted to keep him overnight for observation, but he was going to be okay. No lasting damage.

My legs gave out and, surprisingly, Detective Rheingard caught me, leading me over to a chair.

"All right, Mrs. Lockwood," Detective Rheingard crouched down in front of me. "What the hell happened?"

I reached into my coat pocket and pulled out a small recorder. "It's all there." I looked up at the doctor. "Can I see him?"

"Mrs. Lockwood..." Detective Reed started to protest.

"Are you and Mr. Whitehall willing to come down to the station on Monday and give us a formal statement to go along with what we have here?" Detective Rheingard cut off his partner.

"We'll be there," I promised.

Rheingard's expression softened. "Then go."

The doctor led me into the room where Jasper was laying. He was still unconscious, but that didn't matter. He was alive, and he was going to be okay. That's all I cared about. Everything else was superfluous.

He didn't wake up until he'd already been moved into a private room and it was just the two of us. Only when I saw his eyes open and meet mine did the hand squeezing my heart start to ease.

"What happened?"

His voice was hoarse, and I reached over for the water the nurse had left for him. I held it up and he sipped at it, making a face as he swallowed.

"Short version," I said. "You got your stomach pumped because you're an idiot."

He smiled at me as he reached up and brushed

his fingers across my cheek. "But you're okay."

"Yes, I'm okay." My voice caught and tears ran down my face. "You idiot! You could've died!"

He took my hand, lacing his fingers between mine. "Better me than you." His tone was only half-teasing.

"Don't ever scare me like that again." I wanted to smack him, but instead, I raised our hands and kissed the back of his. "Seriously, Jas, I thought I was going to lose you too."

He squeezed my hand. "Not a chance. I'm not going anywhere." He moved over towards the edge of his bed. "Come here."

I gave him a look that was supposed to clearly say that I thought he was out of his mind, but he just smiled and tugged on my hand. I knew the doctors would probably have a fit, but I didn't care. I crawled up onto the bed and let him tuck me against his side.

"Now," he said. "Tell me everything that happened after I passed out, starting with whether or not you kicked Georgia's ass."

.

Chapter 23

They kept Jasper overnight for observation and I stayed with him. The nurses and doctors seemed to find my refusal to leave Jasper's side endearing, and didn't scold me whenever they came into the room and found me in bed with him.

He was released the next morning and we took a cab back to the vineyard. I'd called Mitchell from the hospital and he'd gone to Georgia's to get Jasper's car, so it was waiting in the driveway when we got home. Mitchell had also left us soup from our favorite restaurant, and a note telling me that he wanted Jasper and me to meet his girlfriend whenever Jasper was feeling up to it. After all, his note said, we were his family. Apparently Jasper's willingness to drink poison for me had gotten rid of any doubts Mitchell'd had about him.

We spent the day on the couch eating soup and ice cream, and whatever else would settle on Jasper's still tender stomach. I'd told him that we'd have to go into the police station on Monday to talk to the detectives about what was on the recorder, and we both knew that most likely meant Jasper would be getting into trouble for the insurance thing, but we didn't talk about it. We simply let ourselves enjoy the fact that we were both alive and everything about Allen's death was finally going to be put to rest.

Jasper closed the clinic for the whole day on Monday, so we got up without an alarm and ate breakfast before heading into the police station. I sincerely hoped that this would be the last time I had to be there. I wanted to go into the new year without all of this stuff hanging over my head.

We were almost there when Jasper broke the silence.

"When would the new quarter begin?"

I blinked, startled. I hadn't even thought about how this would effect my job situation. "I think the week before Christmas. I'd have to check my calendar."

"I was just thinking that if you didn't go back to school until the next quarter began, maybe you could give me a hand at the clinic while I'm looking for a replacement."

I hadn't even considered what Georgia's arrest would mean for the day-to-day running of the clinic. I nodded. "I don't think Principal Sanders would let me come back until the charges were officially dropped anyway, which will take at least a week, and that's if Mr. Henley pulls some strings to get me in front of a judge."

Jasper reached over and took my hand. "I'm sorry."

"About what?"

"About Georgia," he said. "It wouldn't have

changed anything with what happened to Allen, but none of the rest of this would've happened if I hadn't slept with Georgia."

I squeezed his hand. "It's not your fault. You had no way of knowing she'd go so crazy. Besides," I added with a teasing note to my voice. "I have to take at least some of the blame since I was the reason you hooked up with her in the first place."

He gave me a partial smile that said he appreciated what I said, but that he was still blaming himself. I hoped once we were done here, he'd accept the truth and we could put this behind us.

When we arrived at the station, we went straight back to where Detectives Reed and Rheingard were waiting. Rheingard's expression was carefully professional, but Reed couldn't even look at me. It might've been a bit mean of me, but I couldn't help feeling a stab of vindication at his embarrassment.

"We spoke to the prosecutor this morning," Detective Rheingard said. "She'll be contacting your lawyer today to get things set up to have the charges against you dismissed." His eyes slid away, and then back again. "On behalf of the department, I'd like to offer our apologies."

I nodded stiffly. "You were just doing your job." A part of me still believed that, despite how hard they'd been coming at me instead of looking at other aspects of the case. I could be the bigger person here.

"Miss Overstreet gave us a full confession regarding the incidents that took place on Saturday morning," Detective Reed said. "She claimed responsibility for forging the letter, the email, and for sending the falsified medical records to the insurance company."

I felt Jasper stiffen next to me.

"She said that she'd intended to use the letter and email to blackmail you, Dr. Whitehall," Rheingard continued. "Apparently, she believed that if you thought you'd get in trouble with the ethics board, you'd do whatever she wanted."

I could almost sense what Jasper was thinking. Georgia had lied about his role in falsifying the medical records. If he didn't say anything, no one would know the truth. I'd kept the real letter from Allen, but there wasn't any other proof that Jasper had done anything wrong.

"She even told us where she'd hidden Mr. Lockwood's real test results." Rheingard's eyes were on Jasper now. "And you should know, Dr. Whitehall, that part of the agreement Miss Overstreet offered was that her confession was all or nothing. If one part was discredited, then the rest would be too...no matter what we heard on the recording."

"Your secretary seemed quite concerned about your well-being," Reed cut in. "Sort of makes a person wonder how much she might be willing to lie about..."

"The case into Allen Lockwood's death has been officially closed," Rheingard interrupted. "Based on the evidence we have, it's been ruled an accidental death. Our bosses just want this all to go away. So, once we get your statements regarding what happened on Saturday, we can put this whole thing to rest."

I looked over at Jasper and he nodded. I knew he hated the idea of Georgia taking the blame for deceiving the insurance company, but it looked like even a confession on his part wouldn't change anything.

"You do understand that we had to alert the insurance company to the fraud," Rheingard said. "You'll want to speak to your attorney about what that'll mean."

If the only thing that happened out of this was having to give back that money, I wasn't going to complain. It might even ease Jasper's conscience.

"Now, if you'll come with me, Mrs. Lockwood." Detective Rheingard stood. "I'll take your statement, and Dr. Whitehall can give his to Detective Reed. I'm sure the two of you want to get this done and over with."

It didn't take long for either of us to explain how we'd gone to see Georgia to confront her about the letter, and how things had progressed from there. Jasper's statement was a bit shorter than mine since he'd passed out before the police had arrived, so when I came back out into the main room, he was already done.

"What happens now?" I asked as I walked over to Jasper's side. I reached out to take his hand.

"Your statements go into the case file," Rheingard said. "Since Miss Overstreet pled guilty to all of the charges, there won't be a trial. There is always a chance she might recant her statements before the plea deal is official, but I doubt that will happen."

His eyes flicked over my shoulder, his expression hardening. I turned, following his gaze.

May and Gregory Lockwood were standing just a few feet away.

"We received a very distressing call today, Detectives." Aside from her mouth twisting into an unpleasant scowl, May didn't even acknowledge my presence. "You're ruling my son's death an accident?"

"We are," Detective Rheingard spoke up. "There's no evidence to support foul play."

"I want to speak to the captain," May said, drawing herself up to her full, unimpressive height. "I refuse to allow *her* to get away with this."

I was suddenly tired of all of this. I wanted to be done with everything, including the Lockwoods. I could let Henley handle everything with the trust. I didn't even need to be present for the ruling. I was sure I could come up with a good excuse to miss it. There was only one other thing tying me to them.

"Detectives," I said. "What do I need to do to drop the arson charges?"

Jasper's fingers tightened around mine.

"Mrs...uh." Detective Reed looked flustered and I knew it was from the dirty look May was sending his way. "You need the report for your insurance."

"I know." I didn't look at my former in-laws. "But I'm sure we can figure something out. A formal letter from the department stating that you're closing the case because there isn't enough evidence to find the perpetrator, but that you've ruled me out." I gave the men a sweet smile. "I figure it's the least you could do."

After a moment, Detective Rheingard spoke, "I'll take care of it."

"Thank you." I turned towards May and Gregory. "We're done with each other. My attorney will take care of the rest of the trust issue, but I'm not going to be involved. You were never my family. I tolerated you because I loved Allen. Now, I don't have to anymore. Goodbye."

Without waiting for a response, I turned and walked away. Jasper fell in step beside me, not saying a word. When we reached the car, he stopped and pulled me into him, wrapping his arms around me. He kissed the top of my head. "You are so amazing."

I slid my arms around his waist and squeezed. "You and Mitchell," I said. "You're my family."

"And you're mine."

We stood there for a minute until a cold gust of wind blew across us and I shivered. Jasper opened the door for me and I climbed in. He drove over to Mr. Henley's office and dropped me off, saying he'd be back to pick me up in an hour.

Henley was waiting for me, a cup of steaming coffee already on his desk. I took it gratefully as I sank down into the chair. I sipped at the dark liquid, letting it warm me as he filled me in on what I needed to know. While I'd always preferred coffee over tea, recent events had made it so that I doubted I'd ever want to drink tea again.

"Unless Georgia decides to recant her confession before the end of the week, you won't have to deal with anything involved with her case," he said. "You don't even have to be there when she enters the plea. The DA offered fifteen to twenty for all of the charges combined, with her not being eligible for parole for at least ten years."

"What happens if she gets paroled?" I asked. "Or when she gets out?"

"I'll file for a restraining order as soon as I hear anything, so if she comes near you or Jasper, she'll go back to jail," Mr. Henley said. "But that's not something you're going to have to deal with for a while."

"I told the police I didn't want to pursue the arson case," I said. "I know the Lockwoods had something to do with it, but I doubt they'll ever be arrested for it, so I don't really see the point." I set down my half-empty cup. "And I want to be done with them."

Henley gave me a sympathetic look. "I can understand that."

"I do still want to follow through on Allen's trust," I said. "At least through the court date that's already been set. But I don't want to have to be there when the judge rules."

"We can figure out a reason for you not to be there," he said. "Since you've already missed a lot of work this year, maybe saying that you can't miss any more work will be enough."

"Speaking of work." I shifted in my seat. "I'm going to call Principal Sanders to let him know the charges were dropped and that Allen's death has been ruled an accident, but I'm thinking he might need something more from me before he'll let me come back."

Henley nodded. "Not a problem. I'll contact the school and make sure it's all set for you to come back when you're ready."

"It won't be before the beginning of the next quarter," I said. "I'm going to help Jasper at the clinic while he looks for a replacement."

Henley jotted himself a note, his expression sobering as he raised his head. "There's one other thing we need to talk about."

I already knew what he was going to say, but I let him say it.

"The insurance money. Even though Mr. Lockwood's death was officially ruled accidental, Georgia's confession included her saying that she sent false records to the insurance company. That information will need to be turned over to the company, and they're not going to allow the policy dispensation to stand."

"I know," I said. "It's okay."

It was disappointing that I'd have to wait until the trust issue was settled before Jasper could get the money for his clinic, but he had enough to keep it open through the beginning of the new year. And if the judge didn't rule in my favor, there was always the chance that she'd still make the Lockwoods pay out the parts of the trust that had already been earmarked for specific charities, including the clinic. Even if that didn't happen, Jasper and I would find some way to make it work.

Mr. Henley and I talked for the next forty minutes, going over all of the little details of what needed to be done to keep things running smoothly. By the time Jasper came in to let me know he was here, Mr. Henley and I were done. Jasper and I said our goodbyes and headed out to the car.

I frowned at him as I slid into the passenger's seat. He wasn't looking at me and I could feel the tension radiating off of him. Something was up. What could have happened in the hour since I'd last seen him? My stomach knotted with worry.

"Is everything all right?" I asked.

He looked over at me as he started the car. His eyes had that burning look to them, twisting things deep inside me.

"I have a surprise for you."

Chapter 24

After everything we'd been through, I wasn't entirely sure that a surprise was the best way to go about things, but I didn't say it. Once Jasper had said that, I'd been able to relax somewhat because I realized that what I was feeling from him wasn't anxiety, but rather excitement.

Neither of us said anything on the drive home or the walk up to the front door. When we stepped inside, two things hit me together. The first was the smell of something cooking. The second was the scent of pine.

"I picked up some pre-prepared stuff at the store," he said as he took my hand. "I figured neither of us would want to cook, but I wanted us to celebrate with something better than leftovers or mac and cheese. It'll be ready in about forty-five minutes."

My stomach growled. I hadn't realized that I'd missed lunch until now.

"But that's not the surprise." He smiled at me as he led me into the living room.

I stopped two steps in and stared. There, in the empty corner, stood a tree. Not the old fake one, but a real one. Easily six feet tall, its branches full and thick. It was already wrapped in blue and white lights, with silver garland sending little sparkles of color bouncing everywhere.

Sitting on the chair next to it were two boxes and two bags. I recognized one of the boxes as one of mine and Allen's, but didn't know where the smaller one had come from. The bags looked new.

"I brought down your ornaments from the attic," Jasper said as he wrapped his arms around me from behind. "Just yours. None of Allen's or the ones you two had together. And I brought out mine." He kissed the side of my neck. "And then I went out and bought a few that can be ours. Our first ornaments together as a couple."

Tears pricked at my eyes as I turned in his arms, my arms going around his neck. "It's perfect."

"And it's ours." He rested his forehead against mine. "I never want to forget Allen, but I want this to be the start of us making our own memories. The start of our life without all of the baggage we've been dealing with."

"I want that too," I said.

He pulled back enough so that we could look at each other. His expression was thoughtful as he put his hand on my cheek. "I don't want you to regret this. To regret getting involved with me so fast."

"I don't." I hurried to reassure him. "It doesn't feel rushed. It feels right."

"I've been waiting for this life for so long." He touched the corner of my mouth with his thumb and gave me a soft smile. "A life I never thought I'd get to have."

"You have it," I said, turning my head to kiss his palm. "You have me."

"Do I?"

I reached up and ran my fingers through his hair before trailing them down the side of his face. "You do. For as long as you want me."

He took a slow breath and sank down onto his knee. "Forever, Shae. I want you forever."

I couldn't breathe as I watched him reach into his pocket. I was certain if I moved or spoke the spell would break, and I'd discover I was dreaming.

He held up a ring, the diamonds glinting in the fading sunlight. "Will you be mine forever?"

Mutely, I nodded, not trusting myself not to burst into tears. I held out my hand and saw that my fingers were shaking. Jasper wrapped his strong hand around mine, holding it steady as he slipped the ring onto my finger. He raised my hand and kissed the ring. When he stood, I saw that his eyes were glittering with tears.

And then his mouth was coming down on mine and I forgot about everything else. I leaned against him, parting my lips as his tongue teased the corner of my mouth. He took his time, slowly exploring every inch. One hand pressed against the small of my back, the other cupped the back of my head, holding me in place. As if I wanted to be anywhere else.

We were both panting by the time he pulled back. His fingers tightened, massaging my neck as his thumb made circles under my ear. My entire body felt like it was vibrating, cells humming, desperate for his touch. For more.

"You know," he said quietly. "For a while, I wondered if what I felt was just an infatuation, wanting what I couldn't have. That if I finally had you, the desire would fade."

"And?" I raised an eyebrow.

He smiled, his hand sliding around to the side of my neck, thumb pressing against the pulse point there. "And I just want you more every day, every hour." His eyes darkened. "I want you so much it hurts."

"I want you too." I ran my hands down his chest to his stomach. I smiled as I tugged his shirt up. He hissed as my fingers skimmed over those hard, flat muscles. "Sometimes I feel like I'm going to explode, like my body can't contain everything I feel for you."

He cupped my chin and kissed me again, fierce and hard. "I need you." He practically growled the words.

I yanked him against me, a thrill running through me at the feel of him hard against my hip. Arousal flared sharp and bright inside me. I moved my hand lower, cupping him through his jeans.

He swore. Suddenly I found myself on the floor, his body stretched out on mine. I wrapped my legs around him, grinding against him as his mouth came down on mine. His hands were hot as they moved over me, pulling and tugging at my clothes until he managed to get them all off. Judging by some of the tearing sounds I heard, I wasn't sure they'd be wearable again, but I didn't care. I only cared that he was touching me and didn't stop.

"Too many clothes," I breathed into his ear. "I want you naked."

He chuckled, and I moaned as the vibration went through me. He pushed himself up onto his knees and yanked his shirt over his head. He went to his feet, his pants coming off next. I stared up at him, greedily devouring every inch of him. He was so gorgeous. And he was all mine.

His eyebrow quirked up. "What?"

I ran my hand over my stomach and down between my legs, loving how his eyes followed the path. His cock twitched when I slid my finger between my slick folds.

"I was just thinking of how hot you are," I said honestly. "And how you're mine."

He wrapped his hand around his cock, slowly stroking the hard shaft. "I am yours."

He came down between my legs again. He put his hands on my knees and slid them up my thighs. "And you're mine."

I reached down and squeezed his wrist. "Always."

He slid his hands under my hips and raised me up so that my weight was on my shoulders and upper back, his hands supporting me. His eyes met mine and I felt the tip of him brush against me. In one smooth motion, he slid inside and my back arched. I cried out as he filled me, stretched me.

He stayed there for a moment, our bodies locked together, and then he began to move with slow, steady thrusts. Each one went deep, reaching that place inside me that only he could touch. I reached up and put my hands on his, arching my body up to meet him.

His hands slid from my hips to my waist and he pulled me up to him. My butt rested on his thighs as he moved us together. I wrapped my arms around his neck, using his body as leverage to move myself against him, across him. As the pleasure built inside me, my head fell forward. I pressed my face against his neck, moaning as his lips danced across the side of my throat.

"I love you so much," he murmured. "My Shae."

"My Jas." I nipped at his flesh, tasting the salt from his skin. "All mine."

"I've been yours from the first moment I saw you," he said.

He pulled me even tighter to him, my nipples hard points against his chest. We were barely moving, just the smallest back and forth motion that put the perfect amount of friction on my throbbing clit. I flexed my muscles around his cock, and he swore.

"I love you, my Jas." I ran my teeth along his jaw, then nipped at his earlobe. "Now and always." I pressed my mouth against his ear. "Make me come."

He bit down on my neck, hard enough to make me gasp, and then I was on my back and he was over me, pounding into me. I wailed as my climax hit me, every muscle tensing. He kept going, forcing me from one into the next. Or maybe it was the same one, magnified until I couldn't even scream.

My senses were exploding, each one overloading

on a multitude of sensation. The sight of him above me, the feel of his skin on mine. The sound of his voice calling my name. His scent surrounding me. I could taste him.

And then he was coming too, groaning as he pulsed inside me, emptied. I felt him spilling into me, and I reached up, pulling him down onto me. I accepted his weight gratefully, holding him to me even as the pleasure faded and my body gave over to the pleasant fatigue that followed great sex.

Jasper rolled us over so that I was laying on him and reached over his head to grab a blanket from the couch. He pulled it over us, tucking it around our bodies before settling back down with me on his chest.

"I don't know about you," I said as I pressed my lips against his chest. "But I think this should be one of our Christmas traditions."

His fingers massaged my scalp. "What should?" he asked absently.

"This." I flattened my hand on his stomach. "Get a live tree, have sex and then decorate the tree."

He chuckled. "That sounds like a great tradition to me."

I looked up at him. "Does that mean we should start decorating?"

He grinned. "I may need a few more minutes to recover."

I laughed. "Me too." I snuggled more closely to him. "But we have plenty of time."

Chapter 25

Six Months Later

I pulled my feet up onto the couch and tucked them underneath me. I sighed as I looked at the mess around me. School had ended on Thursday, and yesterday had been the teachers' time to clean their classrooms. I'd gotten it all done, not wanting to have to come back in next week. I did, after all, have a lot to do.

Three weeks from today, I was going to be changing my name from Lockwood to Whitehall. It would be one week after the year anniversary of Allen's death, and I was going to be marrying his best friend.

And I knew Allen wouldn't have wanted it any other way.

There were probably some people who thought the two of us were moving too fast, but we didn't care. It was going to be a small ceremony, just the people who really cared about us. Gina and Junie. Mitchell and his girlfriend Brenda. Jasper had invited his parents, but they hadn't said for sure they were coming.

They hadn't been too excited when he'd told

them about our engagement, but they hadn't been opposed to it either, so I was willing to consider that to be a step in the right direction. They would have to be a lot worse than distant to be worse in-laws than the Lockwoods.

I hadn't seen the Lockwoods since that day at the police station. I'd kept to my decision not to continue pursuing the arson case, and I'd let Henley deal with everything to do with the trust. The Lockwoods had tried to drag it out, refusing to adhere to Allen's wishes, even if they received the rest of the trust. That had been my only stipulation to continuing to pursue the case.

Finally, in mid-April, a judge had finally ruled that all of the Lockwoods' claims had no merit and ordered that the trust be released. So Jasper had gotten the money for his clinic, and we'd been able to pay off the loan I'd taken out to cover what we'd originally planned to use the insurance money for.

The clinic was doing well, and Jasper had been able to get enough donations to keep it going without any other financial input. Not that I would've minded using our money, but Jasper insisted that we keep the extra from the trust for the future, just in case.

I still hadn't decided if I was going to go back to school in the fall. Even though Principal Sanders had been agreeable about me coming back at the beginning of the third quarter, I'd ultimately decided against it. Full-time at least.

After talking things over with Jasper and Gina, I'd decided that it would be more disruptive to the students for me to come back than it would be to keep the substitute for the rest of the year. She was a good teacher. Once Jasper had hired his new secretary, I went back as a sub. I hadn't, however, cleaned out my classroom, letting Mrs. Kim use the things I'd bought, hence the reason I'd gone in to help clean up yesterday.

I'd ended up spending the rest of my free time doing something I'd never thought I would've wanted to do. I wrote a book. I'd started it off as an exercise to help me work through everything that happened, but it had ended up turning into something more. A month ago, my agent had called and said she had a publisher interested in my book. They fast-tracked it, and it was due to come out shortly after Jasper and I would be getting back from our honeymoon.

And that was what I was currently working on. Not the book, but rather our honeymoon. The wedding details were more or less taken care of, but Jasper and I had been going back and forth about where we wanted to go. Now I needed to finish making the reservations or we were going to be sleeping in the airport.

Jasper had wanted us to do something big, go to Europe for a couple of weeks. I'd told him that I was fine with us just going to a bed and breakfast up the coast. Finally, we'd talked about it and realized that we were trying to sell the other one on the honeymoon we thought they wanted. Once we'd gotten that out, it had been easy for us to agree that the perfect honeymoon for us would be a week in

Vancouver.

I'd made up a list of places to call and was just reaching for the phone to start making the calls when it rang.

"Hey, Maggie." I leaned back and stretched out my legs, taking care not to kick off any of the papers I had spread out.

"Shae, great news!"

My agent was in her early fifties, but sounded like a bubbly teenager. I sometimes thought that was her secret weapon. People didn't always take her seriously at first, and that often ended up giving her a stronger bargaining position than people realized.

"Really?" I reached behind me and twisted my hair up behind my head.

"I just got a call from Elton in legal, and the publisher received an offer for the movie rights."

I sat up straight. "What?"

Maggie laughed. "That's right. And with the offer made, you're going to clear a million, easy."

I didn't really remember the rest of the conversation, but I must've said the right things in the right places because we ended the call and I found myself staring at the phone. A million dollars. The exact amount of the insurance policy that we'd had to give up.

The amount that Jasper and I could use to do what we'd been dreaming about – start a clinic near the place where it had all started for us, near UCLA. Jasper had hired a couple doctors to help him at the clinic up here, so we'd also discussed getting an apartment down there to stay while we were getting things started. Now it looked like we'd be able to do it this year.

I supposed that answered my question about whether or not I was going to teach next year. It also brought up something else that had been on my mind for a few weeks...

"Hey, babe." Jasper smiled as he came into the room. "Things were slow so I thought I'd come home for lunch." His smile faltered. "Is something wrong?"

I shook my head. "No. Maggie just called." I stood up and gave him a quick kiss. "I just got an offer for the movie rights on my book."

"That's great!" He smiled again as he wrapped his arms around my waist, pulling me against him.

"What's even better is, my cut will be enough to start the clinic in LA." I put my arms around his neck. "So when we get back from Vancouver, we can start apartment hunting."

"What about school?" he asked.

"Well..." I gave him a small smile. "I was thinking it might be a good time to kill two birds with one stone. Take time off to go to LA with you...and take time off to start a family."

His entire face lit up, chasing away any of the lingering doubts I'd had about bringing up the subject. "Really? You don't think it's too soon?"

"No." I shook my head. "I'm tired of waiting. Allen and I waited, wanting to have things happen in the perfect time, but look what happened. We lost what we could've had." I threaded my fingers together behind his neck. "I don't want to waste time anymore."

He stared at me with that intense look in his eyes, the kind that made me think he could see all the way into me.

I shifted uneasily. Had I misread him? "Unless you wanted to wait..."

His mouth came down on mine, hard and fast. "I want to have a family with you." He pulled my bottom lip into his mouth, sucking on it for a moment before releasing it. "In fact." He gave me that smile that made my stomach flip. "I think we should practice."

I let out a squeak as he swept me up into his arms. I laughed and kissed the side of his neck. "Well, they do say that practice makes perfect."

THE END

All series from M. S. Parker

The Pleasure Series Box Set
Exotic Desires Box Set
Pure Lust Box Set
Casual Encounter Box Set
Sinful Desires Box Set
Twisted Affair Box Set
Serving HIM Box Set
Club Prive Vol. 1 to 5
French Connection (Club Prive) Vol. 1 to 3
Chasing Perfection Vol. 1 to 4
A Wicked Lie
A Wicked Kiss
 A Wicked Truth (Release September 15, 2015)
Blindfold (Four part series coming in September, 2015)

Check out all my books at www.MSParker.com
Connect with me on Facebook:
http://Facebook.com/MsParkerAuthor

Acknowledgement

First, I would like to thank all of my readers. Without you, my books would not exist. I truly appreciate each and every one of you.

A big "thanks" goes out to all my Facebook fans, street team, beta readers, and advanced reviewers. You are a HUGE part of the success of my series.

I have to thank my PA, Shannon Hunt. Without you my life would be a complete and utter mess. Also, a big thank you goes out to my editor, Lynette, and my wonderful cover designer, Sinisa. You make my ideas and writing look so good.

About The Author

M. S. Parker is a USA Today Bestselling author and the author of the Erotic Romance series, Club Privè and Chasing Perfection.

Living in Southern California, she enjoys sitting by the pool with her laptop writing on her next spicy romance.

Growing up all she wanted to be was a dancer, actor or author. So far only the latter has come true but M. S. Parker hasn't retired her dancing shoes just yet. She is still waiting for the call for her to appear on Dancing With The Stars.

When M. S. isn't writing, she can usually be found reading– oops, scratch that! She is always writing. ☺

45325794R00127

Made in the USA
Lexington, KY
24 September 2015